PRAISE FOR THE D[

Here are some of the over 100,000 five star reviews left for the Dead Cold Mystery series.

"Rex Stout and Michael Connelly have spawned a protege."

AMAZON REVIEW

"So begins one damned fine read."

AMAZON REVIEW

"Mystery that's more brain than brawn."

AMAZON REVIEW

"I read so many of this genre...and ever so often I strike gold!"

AMAZON REVIEW

"This book is filled with action, intrigue, espionage, and everything else lovers of a good thriller want."

AMAZON REVIEW

CURTAIN CALL
A DEAD COLD MYSTERY

BLAKE BANNER

RIGHTHOUSE

Copyright © 2024 by Right House

All rights reserved.

The characters and events portrayed in this ebook are fictitious. Any similarity to real persons, living or dead, is coincidental and not intended by the author.

No part of this book may be reproduced in any form or by any electronic or mechanical means, including information storage and retrieval systems, without written permission from the author, except for the use of brief quotations in a book review.

ISBN-13: 978-1-63696-162-0

ISBN-10: 1-63696-162-2

Cover design by: Damonza

Printed in the United States of America

www.righthouse.com

www.instagram.com/righthousebooks

www.facebook.com/righthousebooks

twitter.com/righthousebooks

DEAD COLD MYSTERY SERIES
An Ace and a Pair (Book 1)
Two Bare Arms (Book 2)
Garden of the Damned (Book 3)
Let Us Prey (Book 4)
The Sins of the Father (Book 5)
Strange and Sinister Path (Book 6)
The Heart to Kill (Book 7)
Unnatural Murder (Book 8)
Fire from Heaven (Book 9)
To Kill Upon A Kiss (Book 10)
Murder Most Scottish (Book 11)
The Butcher of Whitechapel (Book 12)
Little Dead Riding Hood (Book 13)
Trick or Treat (Book 14)
Blood Into Wine (Book 15)
Jack In The Box (Book 16)
The Fall Moon (Book 17)
Blood In Babylon (Book 18)
Death In Dexter (Book 19)
Mustang Sally (Book 20)

A Christmas Killing (Book 21)
Mommy's Little Killer (Book 22)
Bleed Out (Book 23)
Dead and Buried (Book 24)
In Hot Blood (Book 25)
Fallen Angels (Book 26)
Knife Edge (Book 27)
Along Came A Spider (Book 28)
Cold Blood (Book 29)
Curtain Call (Book 30)

ONE

"You know *Murder She Wrote* was filmed in California, right?"

I said it as I read through the details of a four-bedroom house in Rye, New Hampshire. This one was only a million and a quarter bucks. She didn't answer. I sipped cold coffee from my cup and glanced at where she was sitting at the breakfast table staring at the screen of her laptop. The morning sunlight lay gentle across her face.

"Do we need four bedrooms?" I asked.

She didn't look at me, but she said, "Mm-hmm."

My gaze dropped to her belly. You couldn't see the bulge yet. "Needs a little brother or sister, right?"

"Mm-hmm." This time she said it in more of a rising sing-song.

"If we sell your apartment and my house and the Jag, we can raise a little more than half of what we need."

"We're not selling the Jag, Stone."

"I could probably raise…"

"Nope."

"...fifty or sixty grand..."

"Nope."

"...on the open market."

"Nope." She flopped back in her chair, sighed, and rubbed her face. "It has to be near the sea, the Atlantic, it must have white sand and cliffs, and very green countryside. It's got to be clapboard and have a gabled roof and four bedrooms: one for us, one for each kid, and one for guests who come to visit."

"I am with you on every detail. I just need you to tell me how we raise one and a quarter million bucks without saddling ourselves with a prohibitive mortgage. We are both giving up work, remember?"

She didn't get to answer because my phone rang. The screen said it was the chief. It was my day off, and I thought about not answering.

"Sir, good morning."

"John, I am sorry to disturb you on your day off. It's uh…" He hesitated for a moment. "It's a little odd. Somebody has called me and asked specifically to talk to you. She says she is an old friend."

I frowned. "Oh, what's her name?"

I put it on speaker and laid it on the table. He was still hesitating.

"In fact, she said she was an old *flame*."

I saw Dehan's eyebrows rise. My frown deepened. "What's her name, sir?"

"Jane Morley, the actress."

Dehan leaned back in her chair with her eyebrows all the way up. "Jane Morley is an old flame of yours? You had a thing with *Jane Morley?*"

My frown turned into a wince, and I shook my head. "It was very brief. Sir, did she say what it was about?"

"Yes. It's a cold case. It must be a few years ago now. Her personal assistant was murdered, here in the Bronx, in very odd circumstances. But there was a complete dearth of evidence, and the case went cold."

"I remember."

"You were offered the case, and you refused to take it because you'd had a personal involvement with Ms. Morley."

Dehan was shaking her head. I covered the mouthpiece and said, "It was shortly before we met."

The chief said, "She says she has new evidence, but she will only speak to you. You don't have to take it if you don't want to, John. You can very legitimately—"

Dehan cut across him with her high eyebrows again. "Is there any reason why you wouldn't take it, Stone?"

"No." I said it with a little more firmness than was absolutely necessary. "Have her come in tomorrow morning, and we'll hear the new evidence—if there is any."

He said he'd arrange it, and we hung up.

"How come you never told me?"

I shrugged. "There was nothing to tell. It was a couple of weeks, maybe a month, and frankly, I had forgotten. Are you mad?"

"No, I'm not mad. But it's hard to believe you had an affair with one of America's sweethearts and you didn't remember." She frowned. "Haven't she and Danny Santos been married for about twenty years? Stone, did you have an affair with a married woman?"

I sighed. Before I could answer, she was talking again. "Is

that why you never told me? Mr. Do-It-Right Rectitude had an affair with a married woman? Not *just* a married woman, your honor, but America's Sweetheart Jane Morley!"

"Are you going to shut up any time soon?"

"I am not sure. Depends what you're going to tell me."

"She was the friend of a friend of a friend, and we met at a barbeque given by the friend. We got on well. She was funny and a bit naughty, and I guess I was in the market for a bit of that." I shrugged. "She told me her marriage to Danny Santos was a marriage of convenience arranged by their agents and the studio and that it was open, as long as they were very discreet."

"A marriage of convenience?"

"Yeah. The way she described it to me was that it was like an extension of their movies and the TV show. The fans wanted it, the studio provided it, and she and Danny got paid handsomely for it."

"Huh, so how did it end?"

"Quickly. We had fun, but I was aware it wasn't going anywhere, and she told me she had met a guy who was going to be really useful in her career, and was I the jealous type?"

"And you said you weren't." She smiled.

"Pregnancy has clearly affected your memory, kiddo. I told her I wasn't *French*, and though it had been fun, it wasn't my scene. And that was how we left it."

She nodded a bit, like she was weighing up the data. "And the murder?"

I stood and carried my cup to the table. She had the coffee pot there. I refilled us both and sat.

"This would have been about ten years ago. She had a personal assistant"—I paused to think for a moment—"Katy

Hagan. She'd been with her for years. I'd met her briefly in passing a couple of times. She was very efficient, and Jane depended on her totally."

"Did she know you were having an affair with Jane?"

I smiled at her. She was already on the case. "I guess so. Obviously we didn't discuss it, but I assumed at the time that she did. She knew everything about Jane."

I took a sip of brew, allowing my mind to move back and uncover the events at the time.

"I guess it was a few months after we stopped seeing each other. Katy's body was found in a room at the Seven Nights Hotel on Bruckner Boulevard down by Westchester Creek."

"What the hell was she doing there?"

I nodded. "That was one of the questions they were asking back then. Benini had the case, and he asked me if I had any idea. I didn't. I hardly knew the woman, and I knew nothing about her private life. I can only imagine that she was meeting someone, and either that person killed her or it was opportunistic."

She turned in her chair and stretched out her legs, crossing her boots at her ankles.

"What about the killing?"

I stared at her face a moment, remembering, nodding softly. "Brutal," I said. "The lab said there was very little forensic evidence, but what they could say was that it was a powerful guy. Strong, he beat her up badly, broke several bones, then stabbed her several times with a knife."

"Sounds like a crime of rage."

I screwed up my face and made a "Nyeah" sound. "Yeah, it sounded that way to me at the time and certainly has those features. But maybe *not* because on the one hand, they could find nothing in the hotel room that tied the killer to her, and nobody they spoke to who knew her could think of anyone in her life that was that physically powerful and that intensely involved with her." She grunted, and I added, "Also—and this was a contributing factor to my pulling out of the relationship—show biz people live in each other's pockets. There is no such thing as a private life. They just don't understand the concept. So from what Benini told us, everyone from Jane down to the props manager and the lighting assistant knew everything about Kate's private life, and what they knew was that she didn't have one because Jane and Danny had her going non-stop twenty-four seven."

She screwed up her brow.

"Wait, there is something wrong here." I nodded, but she ignored me and went on. "If Danny and Jane had her going non-stop twenty-four seven, that explains why she had no private life, but it raises a big mother of a question mark over what the hell she was doing at that hotel."

"Agreed."

"The next logical deductive step is that she was there for one of them."

"The next logical deductive step? Where is the wild, foulmouthed Bronx urchin I fell in love with?"

"Shut up. Is Danny Santos big and powerful? He looks regular sized on screen."

"I never met him."

She smiled and winked. "Looks like you are going to now."

I shrugged. "If we take the case."

"Oh, we gonna take the case, blanquito." She said it with

heavy Latino overtones, shifting her head from side to side. "You *know* we gonna take the case."

———

Dehan and I entered Interrogation Room Three with three paper cups of qua-coffee, or what my aunt used to call gnat's pee. As Dehan put the cups on the table, Jane stood and came around the table to take hold of my hands and gaze up into my eyes. At forty, she was still very attractive without the help of surgery.

"John." She said it like it was a whole sentence, with meaning and everything.

I gave her my blandest smile. "Hello, Jane. This is Detective Carmen Dehan, my partner. I was very sorry to hear about Kate." I gestured to her chair. "Won't you sit down?" She backed away a couple of steps, glanced at Dehan, glanced back at me, and sat.

"I was asked to take the case," I told her, "but because we had had a recent personal connection, I refused. Now I understand you have fresh evidence."

She stared at me for a long moment, then looked at Dehan again. "He always was like this. We only dated for about a month, but even back then, he was Mr. Right-and-Proper. It was refreshing for a while, compared with the narcissistic moral cripples I usually date. But you know, I do like a hug and a kiss sometimes and 'Jane, you're as beautiful as ever'—is that too much to ask for?"

Dehan didn't so much chuckle as chortle. Jane turned to me and pointed at Dehan. "She's cute. No hardship having a partner that looks like that, right?"

I watched her and remembered why I had liked her. That made me smile. "When we chew the cud and remember the old times, Jane, it won't be in an interview room. Maybe we can catch up later. But right now we are here because you have evidence relating to a murder inquiry."

She sighed heavily and looked down at the table. She was slim and shapely. Her face was pretty, nice to look at, but her eyes, which were a dark, rich blue, made her somehow more than just pretty. They gave her an odd, captivating beauty.

"All right, Mr. Detective, we'll do it by the book. Yes, I have fresh evidence relating to Kate's murder. You look great, by the way. Time has been kind to you."

"Thank you. I appreciate that. What is the nature of this evidence, exactly?"

She looked at Dehan, sighed again, and shook her head. "You been stuck with him long?"

"A while."

"It turns out that while Kate was my personal assistant, I was receiving letters from someone who might have been a stalker. They started out nice enough, but as time passed and I didn't answer him, they became more"—she paused to think of the word, then said, "intense is I guess the word."

Dehan was frowning and making notes. "Were they threatening? Did they threaten you with violence at any time?"

"Not exactly. I don't think so, anyway. Kate lived at home with me. Danny and I have a very large house, and we found it was just easier if Kate lived in with us. She had no private life to speak of, and this way, she enjoyed a level of comfort and luxury she could never aspire to otherwise.

"As my personal assistant, I trusted her absolutely, and she used to take care of my mail. As you can imagine, I get a lot of fan mail as well as crazy mail, and she would take care of it, filter out the irrelevant, and make sure I got the stuff I did need to see."

I said, "And she never told you about this stalker."

"No. When she was..." She took a deep breath. "When she passed on, for a long time, I couldn't bear to go in her room or look at her stuff. I loved her dearly as a member of the family. But recently, a couple of weeks ago, I started going through her stuff and deciding what to do with it. She had no family except us."

Dehan said, "And you found the letters?"

"There were all sorts. Some she had dealt with, others were waiting to be read and either thrown away or answered or filed. And I found those, all signed, 'Your Man.'"

"Any idea why she kept them?"

"No." She gave her head a small shake. "I can only think that she assumed he was a harmless nut, but something about him made her uncomfortable. She was a very sensible, grounded person, and maybe she thought we might need the letters to get a restraining order if he started parking across the road."

I asked her, "Did you bring them with you?"

She reached down beside her and came up with a plastic grocery bag which she handed to me across the table. "I don't think that's all of them. There seem to be some missing. And there are passages here and there that make me wonder if she got into correspondence with him."

"Like?"

She pulled a folded piece of paper from her purse and smiled at me as she handed it over.

"I've done enough cop shows and movies to know that evidence should be touched as little as possible. When I realized what these letters might be, I made a list of the passages I thought were significant and sealed the letters in a plastic bag. The only prints on the letters should be Kate's, mine, and the writer's."

Dehan nodded. "Good job."

I looked at the list. There were a series of quotes, and beside each quote was a date and two numbers. Jane pointed at them. "The date on the stamp, the paragraph, and the line. I haven't read everything. Like I said, when I realized what they might represent, I sealed them up."

I scanned through them, then read out loud, "'I'd like you to look me in the eye and tell me that,' 'You are standing between two people who were destined for each other. That will have bad consequences.' 'God made something beautiful, and now you are making it foul.'"

Dehan reached across and pointed to a quote near the bottom and read out loud, "'I know you are lying.' That's about as close as you can get to conclusive. If he considered it a lie, she told him something. They were having some kind of a dialogue."

Jane nodded. "That's what I thought."

I folded the paper and put it in the bag with the letters. Dehan leaned out and called a name. A moment later, the door opened and a sergeant came in. I handed her the bag and told her, "Get these copied, then send them to the lab. Label them Jane Morley, the case is Katy Hagan. Tell Joe I'll call him."

She said, "Will do" and left. I turned back to Jane.

"Is there anything else? Did any of this bring back any kind of memories? Did any conversations or comments, any change in her behavior, anything at all come to mind?"

"No, but then I haven't really given it any thought, John. I found these, started reading them, and contacted you."

Dehan asked, "Who takes care of your correspondence now, Jane?"

"I have a secretary."

"Did you ask her if you had continued to receive similar letters after Kate's death?"

"Yes." She nodded. "Of course, it was one of the first things I did. She said she had never seen anything like them and told me I should go immediately to the police. Which I had already decided to do."

I nodded. "Okay, Jane, give us a couple of days. We need to go through these with a fine-tooth comb and have the lab look at them too. After that, we'll be in touch and let you know how things are progressing. Meantime, if you think of anything, just call me or Dehan."

I handed her my card. Dehan slipped hers across the table. "Any developments, keep us posted."

I stood and opened the door for her. She paused a moment to look at me, then smiled. "Thank you, John. It was nice to see you again."

And she walked out.

TWO

We spent the rest of the morning working through the letters, reading them. Things that stood out were the fact that the letters were typed on an old-fashioned typewriter, but, as Dehan pointed out, the address on the envelope was handwritten in neat, elegant script. To add to the apparent inconsistency of those facts, the signature, 'Your Man,' was also typed.

Dehan scratched her head and left a few loops of hair standing up. They made her look cute and were hard to ignore. "Is he stupid," she said, "or is he trying too hard to be smart?"

I shook my head for a bit, then shrugged. "He got somebody else to write the address and post them. We'll probably find an extra set of prints on the envelope."

The content of the letters started out pretty inoffensive but seemed to build in paranoia and narcissism as the letters progressed, particularly when the first suggestions of a dialogue with Kate started to emerge. After a while, I dropped the letter I was reading on the desk and crossed my arms.

"Imagine for a moment you get a serious crush on Hugh Jackman."

"This is before I met you, right?"

"Thank you."

"Otherwise it's just too hard. You know, when you've been with the best…"

"Is this about sticking with the four-bedroom house in Maine plan?"

She smiled and blinked.

"Okay, so you develop a big crush on Hugh Jackman, and you decide to send him a fan latter." She snorted. I ignored her and went on. "You don't know at this stage that you are shortly going to becoming a paranoid narcissist and kill his personal assistant. You're just writing him a nice fan letter telling him how cool he is, right?"

"Okay."

"So why would you type the letter?"

"Maybe I have really ugly handwriting. Maybe I am dyslexic."

"That could make sense, but it raises three more questions. First, who types these days? If you want to send a physical letter instead of an e-mail, you print it. Who has a typewriter? Also, is that why you signed it 'Your Woman' instead of using your name?"

She grunted. "That is odd. If it was just one or the other, you could dismiss it, but all together, it suggests he already knew he wanted to hide his identity."

I nodded. "I think it does. Okay, let's get this stuff to the lab. If we are just a little bit lucky, this guy might have a record for stalking or sexual offenses, and we might just find him on IAFIS."

Dehan gave the look of skepticism. "When he has taken care to type the letters, sign with a pseudonym, and get somebody else to address the envelope? I don't think so, Sensei. But we gotta check, right?"

I made a *whatcha gonna do* face, and we headed out for the Jag, shouldering on our jackets.

We took the Bronx River Parkway as far as the zoo interchange and then turned east onto the Pelham Parkway. It took a little less than an hour, and by midmorning, we were sitting with Joe in his makeshift office drinking coffee from paper cups amid teetering stacks of reports. While we sipped, he examined the letters and the envelopes one by one.

"So let me see if I've got this straight. He types the letters on an old typewriter, he signs with a typed pseudonym and then either writes the addresses by hand or gets somebody else to do it for him."

Dehan answered, "That's what it looks like."

"So I have an observation and a question. My observation is that typewriters are, in principle at least, easier to identify than printers, because of the idiosyncrasies of the keys. My question is, having gone to the trouble of typing the letters, why didn't he type the envelopes? Surely that would be less trouble, and less risky, than involving a third person by getting them to handwrite them."

I nodded. "It had crossed my mind. If he'd used a printer, you might explain it because for dinosaurs like me, lining up the labels or the envelopes can be a pain. But this is a typewriter. You roll it in and you type."

He didn't look at me. He was staring at the letters and

the envelopes, which he had set out side by side. He said, "Yes" in an absent kind of voice.

"You seen something?"

"It may be nothing."

"But it might be something. What is it?"

He raised his shoulders an eighth of an inch. "The envelopes are the kind of thing your aunt in Maine might use. Heavy duty paper, blue with a tiny white fleck. You wouldn't be surprised if they were scented with lavender."

Dehan made a "Huh!" sound.

He went on, "The paper is good quality but nothing special. And his prose—" He shook his head. "It's kind of dry, unfeeling, even when he gets mad. It's totally at odds with the envelopes."

"So he used his mother's envelopes but not the letter paper because it had pictures of kittens on it, or…"

I interrupted, "Letter after letter, for over a year?"

"Or," she went on, "this guy sees himself as subtle and smart and leaves lots of red herrings that lead nowhere."

Joe sighed and sat back. "There could be a million and one explanations. Let's see what we get from the fingerprints. If they don't lead anywhere, it might be worth taking these to an FBI profiler. There are a number of striking incongruities. It's not a lot to go on, but sometimes they can be very helpful."

I asked, "How long will the prints take?"

"Lifting the prints is pretty quick these days; the rest is up to the software. I might have something for you later this morning, but I can't promise."

We finished our coffee, made our way down to the parking lot, and strolled toward the Jag. Dehan linked her arm in mine, and I watched my feet. There was a chill in the air.

"Incongruities," I said.

We stopped by the car, and I looked for a moment at two or three brown leaves that had settled on the grass. The fall was coming.

"Was the killing itself incongruous, Dehan?"

"Yes."

I rested my ass against the door and studied her face. Her cheeks were flushed with the chill, and her eyes were bright. "What was incongruous about it?"

She shoved her hands in her coat pocket and went up on her toes. "The location, the apparent rage of the killer toward an apparent stranger, and the fact that Kate was there at all."

I opened the car door for her, slammed it when she'd climbed in, and went around the hood to climb behind the wheel. There I sat for a moment staring at the tree with its two dead leaves at its roots.

"So let's try a little thought experiment. A big, brutal guy beats Kate up, breaks a few bones, and stabs her several times. For the sake of the thought experiment, we will say that the guy is Jane's fan who has turned out to be a psychotic narcissist. His rage is caused by the fact that Kate will not mediate between him and Jane. So he has persuaded her, we don't know how at this stage, to meet with him. There, in a fit of rage, he beats her and stabs her to death for the purpose of removing the obstacle standing between him and his love, Jane." I paused and spread my hands. "And having done that, he vanishes into thin air and stops stalking her." I nodded for a bit at the tree. "That for me is the most incongruous thing of all. It is even more incongruous than the sensible, grounded Kate agreeing to meet him in the first place." I turned to look at Dehan. "But Joe is right. There are a lot of incongruous features to this case. Everything is wrong, and there ain't nothin' right."

She waited a moment, then added, "I agree, and I know you're getting at something, but I don't know what."

I made the face of ironic humor and eyed her a moment. "Well, if you find out, let me know, will ya?"

She snorted a humorless laugh. "So what now? Maybe we should go talk to Danny Santos. He might know something without knowing it, fresh perspective." She looked out the window, pursed her lips, and spoke with a voice that would have made sandpaper look moist. "She struck me as a woman who thinks she knows everything but misses the subtle nuances."

"Subtle nuances, huh? She struck you that way?"

"Uh-huh." She eyed me. "What? I can't say subtle nuances? All the time I gotta be the Latina for you, papito? What about my soul? What about my personal growth?" She looked away. "I have subtle nuances too, you know?"

I sighed and pulled out of the parking lot, shaking my head quietly to myself. I was heading for the Morris Park exit when my cell rang. I saw it was Joe and pulled over to answer.

"John, where are you?"

"By the Rose Kennedy building, why?"

"You're not going to believe this. We got a hit."

"On IAFIS? So soon?"

"It was very recently added to the system. He's a multiple offender. I'm emailing you the details now."

I thanked him, and a moment later, my cell pinged. I handed it to Dehan. "We got a hit already. Multiple offender, recently added to the database."

She watched me pull out and head for Morris Park again. I glanced at my phone in her hand and then at her face.

"What's the matter? Who is he? What's his name? Where does he live?"

"I can't read and ride, Stone. It makes me seasick. I thought you knew that."

"Sure." I raised both hands. "My bad, I should have realized. We'll stop at Emilio's for ice cream pizza with waffles and Branston Pickle."

"Don't pick on me. And don't tell me I've got hormones or I'll kick your ass all the way to Texas."

We drove in silence for a couple of minutes. Then she sniggered. "You heard about—this is my dad, right? You heard about the Jewish guy who tells his wife they should spice up their sex life?"

"Nope."

She had a sheepish grin on her face that made me laugh. "She asks him, 'Spice it how, Irah? What kind a spice? What you want me to do?' He says, 'Mira, you could moan. When we are making love, you could moan.' 'Moan? You want me to moan?' 'Yeah,' he says. 'You could moan sometimes.' So next time they're makin' it, right? He's givin' it all he's got, and she says, 'Irah, should I moan?' He says, 'No, not yet!' a few seconds later, 'Irah, should I moan yet?' 'No, not yet! Not yet!' 'Irah, should I moan now?' 'Yes!' he says, 'Now! Moan now!' So she starts, 'Such a morning I've had! I couldn't sleep all night with the pain in my knee…'"

She doubled up with her hand on my shoulder, emitting

a high-pitched laugh. I pulled in and parked outside Emilio's as she leaned back, flapping a hand at me. She clung to my arm as we crossed the sidewalk and leaned her head on my shoulder with tears in her eyes.

"God I miss my dad, Stone. He would have loved to see our baby."

I pulled her chair out for her and kissed her head as she sat. I sat opposite. "I know, honey, it's tough. You know I'm here for you anytime you want to talk or—"

"Yeah, thanks, Stone. That's sweet. Means a lot. Listen to me. His name is Bob Newport. He has several convictions going back fifteen years, uh...indecent exposure, soliciting a prostitute, groping a female police officer..." She chuckled, then frowned. "No, that's bad, a police officer should not have to encounter the commission of crimes while performing her duties, right?"

"Dehan."

"Yes?"

"Are you okay?"

"Sure. He lives at 1026 C, Faile Street, in Longwood. Unemployed."

"This guy could be dangerous. You want me to drop you at the station?"

Tears welled in her eyes. "You really care about us, don't you? Me and baby."

I smiled. "Of course I do."

"I'm being stupid. I know. I'll wait in the car. I'm your partner, and I should go in with you, but I should not expose him—her—to risk, right? Maybe you should get another partner."

I was spared having to answer by Emilio ambling over. I

ordered a beer, and Dehan had a green tea. When he was gone, I said, "Listen. The absolute most important responsibility you have now is to look after yourself and the safety and well-being of our baby. You want to stay here with Emilio, you want to go home, to the station or stay in the car, it's all good with me."

"I'll stay in the car."

"If I think he's inoffensive, I'll give you the nod, and you come on in."

"Okay, thanks, Stone."

She looked away, and I pretended to be interested in the grain in the wood on the tabletop. Hormones can be contagious.

THREE

It was a bare brick 1930s construction with three floors plus a basement. Each of those floors had a bow window, which gave the impression of a castle tower running up the side of the house. When it was built in the early part of last century, it was probably a nice family home, with the kitchen and the help in the basement. Now it was four apartments with an old TV and a washing machine decaying on the sidewalk.

I parked in front of the house and climbed the six steps to the porch and pressed the bell labeled C. Behind me, I heard my car door slam. I turned and saw Dehan standing at the foot of the steps. She shrugged as an electronic voice crackled from the door.

"Yes?" It was a high, thin voice. It didn't sound like the Hulk on steroids.

"Mr. Newport? Bob Newport?"

"Yes, who is this please?"

"My name is Detective John Stone from the New York

Police Department. I wonder if you could spare me ten minutes."

There was a long moment of silence, then, "What's it about?"

I sighed audibly. "It's about Jane Morley, sir. I'd rather not have this conversation on the doorstep, and I'm pretty sure you don't want that either. Do you think I could come inside?"

The door buzzed, and as I pushed it open, I was aware of Dehan by my side. She shrugged again as she squeezed past me. "He doesn't sound dangerous, does he?"

"No, but neither did Ted Bundy. Just stay behind me and let me talk to him." Her face told me I was about to get a mouthful, so I added, "*Both* of you!"

She pressed her lips closed and let me climb the stairs ahead of her.

We reached apartment C on the third floor, and I rang the bell. The door opened a couple of inches, and beyond the chain, I saw a small face peering out at me.

"Can I see some ID, please?"

I showed him my badge, and Dehan showed him hers. "I am Detective Stone, this is Detective Carmen Dehan, NYPD, from the 43rd precinct. May we come in and talk to you?"

I saw his eyes fix on Dehan, and after a moment, he closed the door and opened it again without the chain to let us in.

We were in a small passage. On the left was an open door which led to a large room with a bow window overlooking Faile Street. We followed him in. There was a sofa and two armchairs that didn't match. They were old and shabby and had that air of having been bought from a thrift store. There was also a coffee table and a TV, a table by the window with two bentwood chairs, and little else.

He stood beside the sofa. He was maybe five ten, more out of shape than overweight, late thirties with abundant dark hair. He spoke suddenly.

"Should I make coffee? I don't—people don't—I don't see people. Often. I don't know. Sit down?"

I smiled. "That's okay, Mr. Newport. We had coffee already. May we sit?"

I took an armchair, and Dehan took the other. Bob perched on the edge of the arm of the sofa with his hands clasped between his knees.

"You wrote some letters—"

"I write lots of letters. It's a thing I do. I don't work, but I read a lot, and I write a lot of letters. That's not a crime now, is it?"

He straightened with mild indignation as he spoke, but his small hands were still between his knees. I watched his face. His cheeks had colored slightly, and his eyes were bright.

"No, Mr. Newport, it is not a crime to write letters. May I finish what I was going to say?"

"Sorry. I'm a bit quick off the mark. It's the dyspraxia. DCD, developmental coordination disorder. It makes me anticipate, and usually I am right. I'm not clumsy. I seem clumsy, but I'm not. Sorry…"

When he was done, I smiled again. "No problem. The letters I am talking about you wrote a few years back to Jane Morley. Do you remember that?"

"Yes, you said over the intercom. Wonderful actress. I

was desperately in love with her. So warm, and those *eyes!* My God." He sighed.

I leaned back in the chair and crossed my legs. I wasn't sure what I had expected, but this sure as hell wasn't it. "Do you remember the correspondence you had?"

"Good Lord, it was years ago! Must be ten years? Maybe more. And it was hardly correspondence. *I* wrote to *her*. She never wrote back."

"Have you some idea of how many—"

"I think maybe I got on her nerves. I have a range of disorders, you know, and in some cases, I can't hold my focus. If people are too slow, or they take too long to get where I *know* they are going, I lose focus. *Too* slow! *Too* slow!" He laughed and slid off the arm of the sofa onto the seat. "But other times, my focus is *huge,* and I can stay focused for hours, days, even weeks, and that is the only thing I can focus on. So you know, I might have written her a whole barrage of letters and not even realized it."

"You don't remember?"

"Do you remember the letters you wrote ten years ago?" He turned to Dehan. "Do you remember the letter *you* wrote ten years ago?" He gave his head a little shake. "My goodness, you are *beautiful*. You have that glow—" He stopped dead, and his jaw dropped open. "Oh my God!" And then again with more emphasis, "Oh my *God!*" He glanced at me, and in a fraction of a second he had read my face. He clasped his bottom lip with his teeth and smiled.

"Mr. Newport, can we stay on task please? Did anybody from Jane Morley's team ever write back to you? Maybe to ask you to send fewer letters?"

He still had a goofy grin on his face. He gave his head a small shake. "No."

"You never received a message from Kate Hagan, Jane Morley's personal assistant?"

He gave a small laugh, like it was only slightly amusing how hard it was for people to keep up. "So we'll climb back *down* the ladder of abstraction. I think I just answered that question. I never received a message from Jane's team, which includes her personal assistant—about anything."

I sat frowning at him, momentarily unsure which way to go. He took a deep breath that said he was being more patient than I deserved.

"Detective Stone, I fell in love with Jane Morley some ten years ago or more. My various conditions make me a very focused, passionate person at times. Most people despise focus and passion. I wrote to her and bared my heart. I sent her poetry and opened my very soul to her, but either she never received my letters or, as you suggest, her personal assistant *made sure* she never got them. Equally likely is that her agent, Henry Silva, kept them from her, or forbad her to answer. After all, he would not want to share control of his little treasure, would he?"

I gave my head a small shake. "No."

I sat forward with my elbows on my knees. My neurons were engaged in a small riot in my head, and I was having trouble thinking.

"Bob, Mr. Newport, I might want to talk to you again. Do you have a cell where I can call you?"

He heaved another sigh. "But you will please delete it as soon as the case is closed."

"Sure."

He gave me his number and accompanied us to the door. All the way, Dehan was frowning at me like I had started speaking in tongues. But she didn't say anything until we were in the car and I was staring at the bare trees that lined the road. Then she said, "What the hell was that about?"

"I don't know."

"You were done with him? I thought you were just getting started."

"He wasn't what I expected." I turned and frowned at her face. "Incongruous," I said. "I felt like I'd been dropped in the middle of Beijing with a map of Paris."

"I hope you're not being careful on my account, Stone."

"Don't go there, Dehan. That's not it. He was learning more about us and the investigation than we were learning about him." I looked at her again. "He picked up that you were pregnant *and* that I was the father, just by reading us. I was not ready for him, and I was not going into a fight I didn't know how to win."

She was quiet for a moment. "Yeah, he picked that up real fast. So what do we do now?"

"Besides," I added as an afterthought, "I got the feeling he was telling the truth." I sighed. "Now? We go back to the station, get some lunch, and read those letters again. And maybe, maybe make a visit to Henry Silva this afternoon."

She watched me fit the key in the ignition, but before I turned it, she said, "You don't think it was him, do you?"

I turned the key, and the engine roared.

"I don't think anything right now, Dehan. But it did strike me that he is a foot shorter than he ought to be, and the only bones he is liable to break if he hits anyone are the ones in his hands, and the only brutal attack I see him pulling off is the one against the creases in his pillow."

She shrugged as I pulled away. "I hear you, but you and I both know that rage can not only change a person, but give them strength you'd never expect."

"Ritoo Glasshopper speak wisdom words. But Big Stupid Sensei need to regroup and think."

When we got back, Dehan walked down to the deli, and I sat and read through some of the letters again, some from the beginning, some from the middle, and some of the last ones he had written. The phrasing of the earliest ones was recognizable as Bob Newport. It was affected and camp, and left no doubt that he 'adored'—his word not mine—Jane. But as the letters went by and he got no response, the style seemed to change. I sat and scratched my head, staring at one particular line.

...YOUR FAILURE TO RESPOND, even to my most sincere, heartfelt revelations of my own feelings for you, speak of a cold, callous lack of emotion which I never dreamed you would be capable of...

I WAS STILL STARING at it when Dehan came in and put my two roast beef sandwiches and large coffee in front of me. I said, "Listen" and read the short paragraph that followed those lines:

"'Or does it speak of something else? Does it speak of the parasites and carrion-eaters that surround you and imprison you, and insulate you from my words, depriving you of your freedom—and my love? What do they fear? I ask myself, who is reading these words, if not you? Whoever it is, I ask them now, what do you fear?'" I looked up at her. "Does that sound to you like Bob Newport?"

She sat and opened her sandwich. "No." She bit into it, and as she chewed, she asked, "What are you getting at?"

"Is this a case of multiple personality disorder? You read through these letters, and he changes. He starts out as the Bob Newport we met this morning, but he gradually changes. His way of writing changes. He becomes…" I spread my hands and shrugged. "There is only one way to say it. He becomes more *masculine*. I mean, let's face it, if we didn't know that he was obsessed with Jane Morley, we would both have assumed he was not just gay but camp with it. And that's the way he writes in his first letters, like he's writing to Judy Garland. But over the space of a few letters, he becomes increasingly masculine. Is it a dual personality?"

"Jeez, boss, you're in deep water now. I have no idea." We stared at each other while I unwrapped my sandwich and bit into it. Then she said, "Are you serious or just being provocative?"

"I don't know." I swallowed, drank coffee, and asked, "But you know what I've been thinking? I've been thinking that Bob Newport, with his various disorders and phenomenal capacity for focusing his attention, must have an exceptional amount of information on Jane Morley and the people in her inner circle. Did *you* know who her agent was before he told us? I didn't." She grunted, chewed, and watched me. After a moment, I asked, "Do we know what he looks like, Henry Silva? Is he big, powerfully built? Is he as possessive as Bob wants us to believe?"

She chewed, shook her head, and spoke with her mouth full. "Djonow. Lesh foinjow."

FOUR

We didn't call. Dehan found the address of the Gold and Silva Talent Agency in Manhattan, and we took a leisurely drive to West 62nd Street, a stone's throw from Broadway. There we rode the elevator to the twentieth floor and found their offices at the eastern end of a long corridor. The receptionist, an efficient woman with uncompromising blue eyes and white hair, pretended to smile at us and challenged us to tell her what we wanted.

I showed her my badge. "I am Detective John Stone, New York Police Department. This is my partner, Detective Carmen Dehan. We would like to see Mr. Henry Silva."

The smile shifted from fake to compassionate. "I am afraid Mr. Silva is very busy."

"I am sure he is. You don't get an office overlooking West 26th and Damrosch Park without being busy. Just tell him we're here regarding Kate Hagan. He would be very upset if he missed us."

All the fake smiles she had in reserve died and were

replaced by honest disdain. She picked up the phone and pressed a button.

"Mr. Silva, there are two detectives here who want to speak to you. I told them you were very busy... Yes, Mr. Silva, about"—she glanced at me and frowned—"Kate Hagan?"

She listened for a second, hung up, and pointed down a short corridor carpeted in dark blue. "It's the last door on the left."

By the time we got there, the door had been opened by a man who was probably six two, broad-shouldered and, though probably in his early sixties, slim and fit. He had lots of gray hair and a square jaw. His mouth was smiling, but his eyes were frowning. He stood back as we approached and gestured toward a large, mahogany desk.

"Detectives, please come in, sit down." He didn't speak again until he had closed the door. As we sat, he moved behind the desk and sat in his own black leather chair. Then he said, "That's a name I haven't heard for a long time. Kate was very dear to us all. Not just as an extremely efficient assistant to Jane Morley but as a friend. But that was a long time ago. What's this about?"

The frowning smile on Dehan's face echoed the one on Silva's. "You really don't know?" she said. "Jane hasn't told you?"

His eyebrows rose high on his forehead, and he leaned back in his chair. "If your purpose is to worry me, you have achieved it. No, Jane has not told me anything. Please tell me what this is about."

I couldn't think of any reason for him to lie about it, but it was interesting that Jane hadn't told him about the letters. I said, "Jane came to see us this morning. She had found some letters from a fan. It seems Kate had kept them for some reason. When she started reading through them, she realized that the tone of the letters was changing, from pretty standard fan mail to something like aggressive obsession. Did Kate ever mention these letters to you?"

"No..." He screwed up his brow and closed his eyes for a moment. "I mean, this is kind of out of left field, and it was a long time ago. I don't recall anything of that sort."

He looked like he was going to ask a question, but I beat him to it. "Do you recall her ever talking about Bob or Robert?"

He gave his head a small shake. "But I'm not sure I would even if she had. It must be all of ten years."

Dehan asked, "How long have you represented Ms. Morley, Mr. Silva?"

His frown was becoming cautious. "About ten years, or a little more. What are you driving at, Detectives?"

Dehan gave him a blank look, and I shook my head. Apparently, I was the good cop.

"Nothing at all, Mr. Silva. We head up a cold case unit at the 43rd. When Ms. Morley brought in this new evidence, the case was passed to us. We find it helps to start from scratch as far as we can and gather all the facts. So Kate Hagan would have been killed shortly after you started representing Jane Morley?"

"Yes." He seemed to think about it for a moment, then lifted his shoulders an inch. "I suppose that's right. Look, Detectives"—his frown deepened—"am I a suspect in this murder? I had absolutely no reason to want Kate dead. She was a treasure. We all liked her, not least because she kept a tight rein on Jane!"

Dehan's eyebrows shot up. "Oh? Was that necessary?"

Silva sighed. "I mean she made sure she turned up for shooting on time, attended interviews, and all the rest of the stuff actors have to do in order to stay on top."

I scratched my chin. "We have no suspects right now, Mr. Silva. As I said, we are just reviewing the facts. On the night that Kate was killed, she was at a hotel in the Bronx. I know you told the detectives in the original investigation that you had no idea what she was doing there."

"That is absolutely correct, and I still haven't."

"Is there anything you can tell us about that night, or the hours leading up to it?"

He gazed for a moment at the plate glass window overlooking West 26th, the south end of Riverside Park and the great, dark mass of the Hudson beyond. He seemed to surprise himself and said, "As a matter of fact, I can tell you something, yes. Because that night I was at a gala dinner with Jane and Danny. It was 26th October, 2002, Jack Roch's birthday, and everyone was there—Billy Crystal, Christopher Walken, Julia Roberts. If you were somebody, you were there."

"Kate wouldn't have been there?"

He looked like he thought he should be embarrassed but wasn't. "She was a lovely woman, but she was an assistant."

Dehan was making notes and said to her pad, "Not somebody."

"That's right, Detective Dehan, not somebody. That's how it is in show biz. You are either somebody or you're anybody."

I asked, "What time did the gala start?"

"Seven? That's the time these things usually start. We probably arrived at half past."

"You arrived together? The three of you?"

He gave it some thought. "Yes, Danny had a Rolls Royce. I think he had it on semi-permanent loan from the studio in Los Angeles. He could get away with things like that back then. So he and Jane picked me up from my apartment, and we made a grand entrance at the Plaza on West 59th. That's where the gala was."

Dehan said to her notebook, "And you arrived half an hour late."

"Stars like Jane and Danny, America's sweethearts, cannot arrive on time. They have to arrive at least half an hour late. More than that might be offensive to the host, depending on who he is."

"Right. I'll bear that in mind when I get invited to Robert de Niro's birthday party."

He didn't laugh. I asked him, "Until what time did you stay?"

He bunched his lips, trying to remember. "A man like Jack is extremely influential in the industry. He pulls a lot of weight and generates a lot of high-value work. So you don't want to be among the first to leave. What you want is to be invited to the private party after the gala."

"Was that what happened?"

"Yes. Me and Danny and Jane went back to his penthouse after the gala. Julia was there, Billy, I can't remember exactly." He gave a self-deprecating laugh. "The usual suspects!"

Dehan gave him a look that said she didn't think that

was an appropriate kind of joke. I asked him, "What time did you leave the party?"

"I don't recall exactly, but the sun was rising. Danny and Jane dropped me at my apartment, and they went on home. It was later that day that Danny called me and told me they had found Kate in this bizarre place."

Dehan raised an eyebrow at him. "Bizarre place?"

"That hotel in the Bronx."

"Is it the hotel or the Bronx you think is bizarre, sir?"

His cheeks colored slightly. "No, I mean, there is nothing bizarre about either place. I mean it was a bizarre place for her to be."

I asked, "It was Danny who called you?"

"Yes. Poor Jane had been sedated. She absolutely adored Kate. She depended on her totally. It was weeks, maybe a few months, before she was back to anything like her old self."

I remembered Benini talking about the state she was in and the articles in the press. Silva hesitated a moment and spread his hands. "Is there anything else, Detectives? I really am very busy."

I didn't move for a moment, then leaned forward with my elbows on my knees. "Mr. Silva, this may be a cold case, but it is still a murder inquiry, and sometimes we have to intrude into sensitive and uncomfortable areas. So forgive me for the question I am about to ask, but I do have to ask it. Did your relationship with Jane Morley ever become intimate? I mean were you ever lovers?"

He was going to deny it but hesitated just a second too long. Instead, he sagged back in his chair and sighed.

"It would be absurd to deny it. Yes, we were briefly lovers

after we first met before she became my client. But it didn't last. It was just a few weeks."

Dehan was arching her eyebrow again. "It didn't last? With Jane Morley? She's every guy's dream."

Silva repressed a laugh. "Yes, Detective Dehan. That is undeniable. But as it turns out, dreams are sometimes best left as dreams because the reality can be disappointing. And now, if there is nothing else, I really must insist."

I nodded. "Sure." I stood and regarded him a moment, wondering how he would respond. "Mr. Silva, we may need to talk to you again. Have you got a cell where we can contact you directly?" He took a deep breath and looked unhappy. I said, "We won't use it unless we have to, and we will delete it once the case is closed."

He made a show of trying to smile. "Of course." He picked up a card from a small box on his desk and handed it to me. I thanked him, and we made our way toward the door, but as Dehan opened it, I stopped, turned, and walked back toward the desk a few steps.

"Mr. Silva, this may sound like an impertinent question, and I don't blame you if you refuse to answer it. But do you mind telling me what it was, exactly, about Jane Morley that disappointed you?"

The astonishment was writ large on his face. For a moment he foundered, then scowled. "The question is not only impertinent, it's offensive in the extreme! And I do refuse to answer it! How dare you ask such a question?"

"If you would humor me, the question may actually be relevant to the motive for Kate's murder."

"*What?*"

I nodded a few times, like I understood his outrage. "Let

me rephrase the question, Mr. Silva. Was it her intellect, her conversation, or her behavior that disappointed you?"

His face flushed with anger. "Certainly not! Now get out of my office immediately! My attorney will be contacting your chief with a complaint in the strongest possible terms!"

I offered him my blandest of smiles. "I apologize, Mr. Silva. I think you must have misunderstood my question. I withdraw it, and if I have offended you, you have my unqualified apology."

All the way down in the elevator, Dehan was silent. She was silent as we crossed the lobby, and she was silent in the cold sunshine as we crossed the sidewalk and climbed into the car. Then, as I turned the key in the ignition, she said, "You want to explain that last question?"

"Sure." I pulled out and headed toward Amsterdam Avenue. "Do you ever get a flash?"

"I think I might be about to get one now."

"I'm serious, Dehan. I'm serious, like a hunch, but sudden."

"A flash of hunch?"

I grinned at her. "If you like. A flash of hunch, yeah."

"And what was your flash of hunch? The Jane Morley Fan Club comparing notes on how good she was in bed?"

She was trying hard to smile, but the two red dots on her cheeks said she was losing the fight.

"No, come on! Of course not. You know me better than that, Dehan. It was when he said it had only lasted a few weeks. I heard myself telling you that this morning, in almost the same words." I glanced at her. She was studying my face with curious eyes. I said, "Do you ever get that thing where it's like your unconscious mind is working too fast for you to keep up?"

"Yeah, I guess so."

"It was like that. As soon as he said it, I knew it was significant."

"It was significant that they didn't have the chemistry in bed?"

We were moving north, taking it easy. Was that what I had meant? "Kind of."

Her face said she'd had a flash of her own. "She wasn't good in bed with you, either, was she?"

I shook my head. "Nope."

"And you think that means something?"

"That's putting it too strongly, Dehan. But in that moment, I felt it was significant. Let me see if I can put it into words."

"Please do."

"Okay, we start from the fact that everything in this case is incongruous, right?" I looked at her, and she nodded. She still looked like she wanted to kick my shins. "And the more I think about it, the more incongruous it becomes, starting with the fact that the way all the evidence points, it should have been Jane who was murdered, not Kate."

"Whoa! How—?" She stopped dead, then said, "The stalker was stalking her. The agent Bob hinted at was trying to control Jane, not Kate, and his affair was with her, again, not Kate…"

"And the woman who is having a string of affairs in her open marriage is Jane, not Kate. Everyone agrees that Kate had no social life, no lovers, no affairs. All she did was work. Silva himself described her being in that hotel as bizarre. But if Jane had been found in a hotel in the Bronx, that would not have been bizarre to anyone who knew her."

"Okay." She nodded slowly, pushing out her lower lip. "I hear you. It's kind of weird, like the victim should have been Jane, but Kate did even that for her. But how does that tie in with her being a disappointing lover?"

I took a deep breath. "I can't put my finger on it. You came close in the office when you said she was every man's dream."

"And he replied that—" She closed her eyes and quoted, "'Dreams are sometimes best left as dreams because the reality can be disappointing.'"

"Right. She is America's sweetheart, a living dream, yet her marriage to her husband is a failure, she has affair after affair, but apparently nothing satisfies, and she never fails to disappoint."

She rubbed her face with both hands. "So what are we saying here, that she arranged a meeting with some guy at the Seven Nights but didn't turn up because she was going to Jack Roch's birthday party and sent Kate instead? And the guy was so sick of being disappointed by her that he beat Kate to death?"

"Well, when you put it like that..." I trailed off.

"But," she said after a moment, "I know what you mean. It *feels* like there is something there."

"Right. But I can't get it."

We drove in silence toward the Harlem River. After five minutes, as we were approaching the water, she said suddenly, "So Jane Morley was a letdown in the sack, huh?" I grinned but didn't answer. "So how would you rank us? How do I rate, huh? How does the goddess *Jane*

Morley rate against me Carmen Dehan of the Bronx? Huh?"

I shook my head, then shrugged. "If she is Britney Spears, you are Sarah Vaughn, the Divine One. How does Justin Bieber rank against Mozart? How does Joe Knuckles rank against the Angel Gabriel? How does Spam rank against fresh bison sirloin, frozen cheesecake against genuine, homemade Mom's blueberry pie, a drizzling Monday morning at Hunts Point to dawn in the Wind River Mountains? How can you compare the profane with the divine? There is no comparison."

I realized I had been rambling half to myself, and when I looked, I saw she had pulled up her collar, had an idiot grin on her face, and was mopping the tears from her cheeks with a wet handkerchief.

FIVE

I had retrieved one of two evidence boxes from the storeroom, and it now sat between us on the desk. Dehan was staring at the crime scene photographs, and I was going methodically through Kate Hagan's bank, credit card, and phone records for the week before the murder.

"He was big…"

Dehan's voice intruded gently on the numbers I was looking at.

"Huh…?"

She raised her shoulders slightly and spread her hands. "He was big."

I nodded once absently. "Joe and Frank both agreed that he was a strong man." I turned back to the numbers.

"Silva is big." I ignored her, but after a moment, I felt her eyes on me. "He's big, about the right size, and had a possible motive."

I sighed and met her eyes. "I have two answers for you, Dehan. The first is what motive did Silva have for killing

Kate? He *might* have had a motive for killing Jane, but why Kate? What kind of threat was she to him?"

She pointed at me across the table. "Because she was going to spill the beans about him and Jane."

"What reason would she have for doing that? Jane had affairs like other people had coffee."

"First thing in the morning?"

"Several times, and then casually with friends several times a week. I think that's where the metaphor peters out. Kate must have been used to Jane's affairs. What would make this one special? Also, why would he care?"

But even as I said it, I saw my mistake. She put it into words.

"Uh-uh. Remember that Jane Morley and Danny Santos *are* America's sweethearts, even now. Everyone who believes in the girl-next-door, Mom's apple pie, and good, clean values *loves* America's sweethearts. Now it turns out she, the symbol of all that is good in the American woman, has been screwing around with her agent? This is not like Clinton playing doctor in the Oval Office or Trump sticking his hand up some dame's skirt. People expect that, and their fans even admire it. No, this would be a direct attack on Middle America's deeply held moral values. It could cost them millions, and it would cost *him* fifteen percent of everything it cost Jane and Danny."

"Yeah, I see that. But it doesn't answer what motive Kate would have. Any loss of income Jane suffered would impact her. She would even lose her job."

She leaned back in her chair, narrowed her eyes, and wagged a finger at me.

"Stone, hang on there. Would it? Let's think this

through, and let's think about the people involved. According to her file, Kate Hagan was in her late thirties. From the photographs, she was not unattractive, and from the way she managed what must have been a difficult and demanding job, she must have been smart."

"Okay, that all makes sense."

"Now suddenly, one birthday, she sees the first ominous looming of her menopause rise over the horizon."

"Huh."

"And she begins to ask herself questions. She has devoted her adult life to the present and future wealth and happiness of Jane and Danny, and now Silva. But what is to become of her? What is her future? Does anybody even care? All those people she has supported just take her for granted. What will happen when she is too old, too tired to carry on? They'll ship her off to a home to die alone and neglected."

"Okay, this is interesting."

"So what does she do? What does this intelligent, able woman who knows *everything* about Jane Morley do? She doesn't jeopardize her position with Jane. No way. She goes to Silva, who is raking in fifteen percent a year from some of the richest talent in Hollywood and New York. She goes to him and says, 'Pal, how much are you prepared to pay in order to protect your investment?'"

"She blackmails him."

"Right. And he arranges to meet her in a bizarre place like the Bronx and kills her."

I nodded for a bit. "It's a really attractive theory, but my second point is that he has an alibi."

She made a derisive face. "An alibi is only as good as its witnesses. And a witness is only as good as the alcohol he has not drunk. You heard what Silva said. They went from the gala to the party and left at dawn. There must have been hundreds of slightly drunk people at the gala, and whoever made it to the party was too busy sniffing coke and getting laid to notice who came and who went."

"Boy, at one stroke, huh?"

"Am I wrong? Also, what's to stop him arranging a hit?"

I smiled. "This might come as a surprise, Dehan, but most people don't know how to do that."

"You want to lay a bet? Twenty bucks says he has connections in the Mob."

"Has he?"

"Would I bet if I didn't know already? I checked. He represents Leo Negroni, whose uncle is Papa Negroni of Noo Joyzee."

"That's a pretty big leap, and all of it sprung from supposition."

"Sure, I agree. But right now, what else have we got? Questions. Questions like, what the hell was she doing in that hotel room? The door was not forced, so two gets you twenty she knew her killer. So question two, who, or as you would say, whom was she meeting? And what were they doing that they had to go do it in the bizarre Bronx?" She pointed at me. "Supposition or not, I challenge you to come up with a better theory that covers all the facts."

I had to admit she had a point. I looked down at the numbers on the page in front of me. "She called the hotel a couple of days before and booked a room."

"Did she call Silva?"

I gave a small laugh. "Numerous times. But then she would, wouldn't she?"

She sighed and stood. She placed her hands on the small of her back and stretched, and suddenly, for the first time, she looked pregnant. I was going to say something about taking her home, but she pointed at me.

"Either this killer is the luckiest son of a bitch on the planet and has committed the perfect crime by pure chance, or he is *real* smart."

I looked back at the pages in front of me. "She called him," I said. "She received several calls in the days before she booked the room. I have traced them all. There's an airline, several stores, Tiffany's, a hair salon, a manicurist, and three calls from Silva. Now that tells us something. If—*if*—the killer called her, it was Silva. But if it was not Silva, then she called her killer and arranged to meet him."

She thought about it a moment, then nodded. "Yeah, that makes sense. So we need to trace all the numbers she called in the days before she booked the room, and in the days after she booked up to the time she was killed."

"That's a lot of numbers, and a lot of them might be discontinued." I smiled at her. "You want to do that? It'll keep you off the streets. I was worried a couple of times today."

She gave a nod that was more reluctance than agreement. "Yeah, I guess. What are you going to do?"

"I'm going to go and talk to Danny Santos. He's a big, strong guy. We've been talking about Jane being a disappointment, and people getting tired and frustrated with being taken for granted by her." I gave my shoulders a little hitch. "Well, when you think about it, we only have Jane's word for the fact that Danny was a willing participant in this open marriage."

She laughed. It was humorous but had a touch of irony. "Isn't that an observation you should have made ten years ago?" I grimaced. She went on. "Even so, Stone, once again, that would provide a motive to kill Jane, not Kate."

"Yeah, I know, and that keeps nagging at me. I know it means something, but I can't pin down what. Either way, it's not impossible to imagine a situation where Danny is trying to get information out of Kate, Kate is loyal to Jane and refuses to cooperate, and he ends up slipping into a rage."

She showed me a skeptical face. "They can't discuss that at home, while Jane is out making hay with one of her unsatisfied boyfriends? They need to book a hotel room in the Bronx?"

We both stared at each other because we had both had the same thought at the same time. I spoke first.

"All those years living in the same house, never feeling the need to socialize or seek a boyfriend or a husband."

"And neither of them ever complaining or disapproving of her affairs."

"Because they had each other."

She sat back in her chair. "Danny and Kate, hiding behind his wife's indiscretions."

I scratched my head. "It still leaves us the question, if they have been living together all these years, why now the hotel?"

She nodded. "The hotel room and the murder are both for the same reason."

"What has made them now meet privately, secretly? What has happened that will now lead to her death?"

"One of them has had enough. It's the Jane Morley syndrome. One of them has grown tired and unsatisfied.

They want to shut down America's sweethearts and get married, live a normal life."

I grunted. "She wants them to break up so she can marry Danny, but he stands to lose too much. She threatens to expose the whole affair, and he kills her. Or—"

"He wants to break up with his wife so he and Kate can marry, but we have already been told she is down to earth and practical, and she tells him no way. He, rejected and frustrated, loses it and kills her."

I laughed. "So we have gone from having nothing to having four working hypotheses."

"Four?"

"I haven't discarded Bob's multiple personalities. There is something very wrong with that whole setup."

Dehan shook her head. "Nah. That's a blind alley, Stone." She held up a finger. "Number one, Silva, number two, Kate wants marriage and Danny kills her, number three Danny wants marriage and Danny kills her, number four Bobby has a narcissistic sociopath alter ego."

I stood and arched an eyebrow at her. "Ask yourself a question, wiseass. Of those three suspects you named in those four scenarios, which ones have a really good alibi comprising *hundreds* of witnesses for that night? And which one has no alibi and saw Kate as a significant barrier to his relationship with Jane?"

"I say to you, pfui!" she said, reaching across for my sheets of numbers. "Are you a dunce, sir? Does he go and kill Kate to remove this alleged barrier, and then fail to capitalize on it by pursuing the object of his affections?"

"You do that really well."

"Thank you. I figure soon I'll be as big as Nero Wolf, so I may as well learn to talk like him."

"One thing you forgot to take into account, Dehan."

"What?"

"Maybe he actually got to hit the sack with Jane and lost interest."

I left her staring out of the window with a wince fixed on her face.

In the car, I called Jane.

"Hello, darling."

"Jane, I need to talk to Danny."

"What on earth for?"

"Jane, I am going to tell you something, and I am going to ask you not to put me in this situation again."

"Tell me something? Tell me what?"

"I am a homicide detective investigating a murder. I do not need to explain my investigation to you or anyone except my chief and my partner, and perhaps a judge. Don't ask me to explain to you why I want to interview Danny Santos or anybody else."

She was very quiet, then, "I'm sorry. That has put me firmly in my place."

"What happened between us happened a long time ago, Jane, and I would like us to be friends. But don't get the idea that I am now somebody whose strings you can pull. Until this investigation is over, I am a cop and you are a witness. You need to understand that."

"You have made it very clear."

"So will you arrange for me to meet Danny, or shall I go through Silva?"

"I'll arrange it. When do you want to see him?"

"Now."

"Good Lord! Were you always this intense? I remember you as fun!"

"Now, Jane. Is he at home?"

"Yes, we both are, at the brownstone on West 88th."

"I'll be there in half an hour. I want to talk to him alone."

"My goodness you can be unpleasant when you want to be."

"There are a lot of people who would agree with you, Jane. Many of them are behind bars. Tell him I'm on my way. And don't be there when I arrive. We'll talk later."

I hung up, fired up the big cat, and headed for Manhattan's Upper West Side.

SIX

It was one of those streets that could only be in New York. It was lined with oaks and plane trees that partly obscured the procession of elegant 1930s stoops. Most of the houses were four-story with hefty bay windows on the second floor, displaying elaborate stucco on their underside. The majority of the stoops led straight down to the sidewalk, but Jane and Danny's was part of a pair with strong elements of art deco, where the stoops made right angles decorated with delicate curves and spirals.

I climbed the stairs and pressed the bell beside the big oak door. I didn't hear anything, and nothing happened. A minute passed, and I was about to ring again when the door opened. Jane was standing there looking exquisite in a dark blue coat. It hung open over a white lace blouse, and I could see a string of pearls around her throat.

She stood staring at me for a long moment, then stepped to within an inch of me and placed both her palms softly on my chest. She stared at my buttons, then raised her eyes to look into mine. Very quietly, she breathed, "I despise you, and yet…"

She trailed off, slipped past me, and ran delicately down the steps to the sidewalk. Then she was walking briskly away.

I stepped inside to the large, dim entrance hall. The door closed behind me, cutting out the light from the street. The floor was different shades of toffee marble arranged into geometric shapes. On the left, an elegant mahogany staircase carpeted in red rose to the upper floors. At its foot there was a set of large walnut doors. On the right, another set mirrored them. Beyond it, a corridor was lost in shadow.

I called out, "Hello? Mr. Santos?" My voice echoed for a moment and then was lost in the darkness. I waited, and after what seemed like a long time, the doors on my left opened, and he stood looking at me.

He was taller than he seemed to be in the movies. He was in his late fifties but still vigorous and erect with broad shoulders and a handsome face. It was a face that didn't look real friendly in that moment.

"Detective Stone?"

I pulled my badge, and my steps echoed as I crossed the marble floor.

"Detective John Stone, NYPD. Thank you for seeing me, sir."

The smile was mildly ironic and surprised me. "Given that you have slept with my wife on something like a dozen occasions, I think Danny would probably be more appropriate than sir. Come in."

I stepped into a long, spacious room with a rich burgundy carpet, a stone fireplace, a heavy desk, and burgundy leather furniture. The walls were lined with books, and French doors stood open onto a large lawn.

He gestured at the sofas. "Please take a seat. Can I offer you a drink?"

"I'm afraid I'm on duty."

"I won't tell."

Clearly that closed the argument because he poured two glasses of whiskey from a decanter and handed me one. We sat on either side of the fireplace. He toasted, and we sipped. As he set down his glass, he said, "I'm not sure what you want to discuss with me, Stone. I told what little I know to the detectives ten years ago."

The whiskey was excellent, and I took a second sip.

"There are aspects of this case which I find mystifying, Danny. I guess what I would like is to discuss those points with you and see if you can cast any light on them."

He spread his hand and gestured at me, inviting me to go ahead.

"I imagine you knew Kate quite well."

"Lord yes, she was family. She'd lived as one of us for years. She was housekeeper, Jane's personal assistant, friend, confidant. You name it."

I nodded. "And from what Jane has told me, she had practically no private social life."

"None to speak of. To be honest with you, Stone, Jane gave her no *time* for a social life. But that seemed to suit Kate. I suppose a psychologist would say she was insecure or something, but she had a very rich social life accompanying us to events and parties and things, and on the other hand, she seemed to have no interest in having any kind of sentimental or romantic life."

I studied his face a moment and found only bland honesty. I reminded myself he was an actor and told him, "Henry Silva told us this morning that Kate had not been invited to the gala the night she died."

He raised his shoulders slightly. "That is not exactly correct. The three of us had been invited to the gala. It was just a given back then, if Jane was invited then Kate went too. Jane was very dependent on Kate. But Kate hadn't been invited to the private party afterwards at Jack's place." He threw back his head and laughed suddenly. "Kate was a wonderful person and could be very dry and witty, but she wasn't fun. Not what is considered fun in Hollywood. She preferred not to come along to those parties."

"So what reason did Kate give for not going?"

"She said she was feeling very unwell and asked us to go without her. Jane was going to stay with her, but we both prevailed upon her to go to the party. Jack is a very influential man, and it pays to stay in with him."

I sighed heavily. "There is very little doubt in our minds, Danny, that Kate had arranged to meet her killer at that hotel. She booked the room herself. Now you have said yourself that her social contacts were limited to her immediate circle. I'm sure you'll see that it stands to reason that the person she arranged to meet at the hotel either made that arrangement with her by telephone or in person."

He was frowning as he listened and nodded. "I'd say that was indisputable unless he was telepathic."

"We are going through her telephone records as we speak. Her calls are to a pretty narrow group. The fact is, Danny, in the days running up to her death, it is almost certain that you saw her speaking to her killer."

He went the color of pale wax. It was something you couldn't fake, only I couldn't tell what it meant. He breathed, "What are you saying, man?"

"Think it through. The three of you live in each other's pockets. Either you or Jane are with her practically all day. She simply hasn't got the time—you used that word yourself—to develop any kind of relationship outside the circle that you and Jane move in, much less the kind of relationship you get killed for. She booked the hotel room a couple of days before she was killed. So she arranged to meet someone in that room a couple of days before that." I pointed at him. "Somewhere in your memory of those days, conscious or unconscious, is Kate talking to the man who killed her."

I gave him a moment and watched his eyes. His gaze was abstracted, like he was searching his memory. I went on.

"He was a big man, strong, strong enough to break her bones, with big hands and big feet. Have you any recollection—"

His pupils contracted suddenly, and he stared at me. "But that's… But the only man like that, that she had any protracted contact with, was—but that's impossible. We were all three together all night…"

He trailed off, and his eyes seemed to glaze.

"Who?"

"Well, Henry. Henry Silva. But we collected him from his apartment, and we were together all night."

"It was a big gala with hundreds of people. Are you one hundred percent certain he was there all the time?"

He looked distressed, staring at the floor, like he might find more accurate memories there. "It was ten years ago, but I am certain, I mean, how long would he have been gone?"

"If he took the FDR"—I shrugged—"ten miles. If there wasn't much traffic, call it fifteen or twenty minutes, he'd have to be gone an hour." I sat forward. "I don't want you to point the finger at anyone, Danny, and I am not looking to prosecute an innocent man. But somebody killed Kate, and one thing that everybody agrees on is that she had no social life—or any life at all, for that matter—outside her life with you. That leads irresistibly to one conclusion. Her killer was from your circle." I paused. "Now I want you to think very carefully. Is it possible that at the gala, or the party, you might have lost sight of Henry Silva for an hour?"

He thought about it for a long time. So long I began to think he had spaced out, but eventually he took a deep breath and spoke.

"Stone, I don't know. We were drunk, later we were a bit stoned. With that kind of wild partying, you lose track of time, and you know Jane and I have an open relationship, so we certainly aren't in each other's pockets." He sighed. "She and Henry had been close. I may..." He trailed off. "I may have thought they had gone off together. But it was ten years ago, and I had no idea at the time how important it would be."

"Let me ask you a question, Danny. You say you have an open relationship and she might have gone off with Henry. How about you? Did you go with anyone?"

He was quiet a moment, looking at the floor. "Yes," he said. "I was with a couple of girls Jack had brought along."

"So while you were with these girls, you had no idea

where Jane and Henry were, even though you had come together."

"That's true."

"You didn't mention this at the time."

"No." He had gone ashen. "You have to realize, Stone, if it had got out that Jane and I slept around, the consequences…"

I drained my glass. As I set it on the table, I said, "I have one more question, Danny. You have been very helpful, and I realize how difficult this has been for you. I can promise you that we will treat this with the utmost discretion."

"Thank you."

"The reason Kate had no sentimental life, no social life outside of her life with you, was that because she was in love with you? Were you and she in a sentimental relationship with each other?"

He stared at me like I'd started speaking to him in ancient Greek. Then he narrowed his eyes and said, "*What?*"

I gave him the face of irony. "Don't overdo it, Danny. We both know you had an open relationship with Jane. Kate was not unattractive and might well have offered you everything you were missing in your official marriage. She was there, and you said yourself you were fond of her. Is it such a reach to wonder whether you and she slipped into a relationship that gave you both more than you got from your wife?"

He screwed up his brow and closed his eyes. "My God, you're serious."

"Of course I'm serious. Come on, Danny! Kate was murdered. This is not a game. Somebody beat her and stabbed her to death. Did you and she have a sentimental or sexual relationship?"

"*No!*" He gave his head several little shakes. "And surely you don't suspect *me* of killing her?"

"Maybe I do and maybe I don't. Give me one good reason why I shouldn't."

"I was at Jack's party, for one!"

"Yeah, like Jane and Henry Silva. You're all three each other's alibis, only now it turns out you didn't have eyes on them all night. And if you didn't have eyes on them, they didn't have eyes on you, either."

He sagged back in his chair. "Dear God, this has turned into a nightmare." He covered his face with his hands, then took them quickly away to reveal wide, staring eyes. "I mean, in one breath you say I loved her and maybe I killed her! If I loved her, why would I kill her?"

"Did you? Did you love her? Did you kill her?"

"No! And no! I loved her as a friend, as a member of the family. And of course I didn't kill her! That is madness! She was a dear, harmless woman. And believe me, Stone, Danny Santos in an open relationship in New York and Hollywood lacks for absolutely *nothing!*"

I put an ironic smile on the side of my face. "Okay, if you say so."

He sighed. "I have played enough detectives, Stone, to know that you have to ask these questions. I don't resent it, but believe me. There was nothing between me and Kate. If there had been, Jane would have noticed. It would have been impossible to hide. And she would never have tolerated it."

For some reason, that seemed to make sense. I leaned forward with my elbows on my knees again and looked him in the eye.

"In that case, Danny, you have to come to terms with the

facts that in the days leading up to the gala, in the week or two prior, the chances are very high that you saw Kate talking to her killer."

He watched me get to my feet.

"Thanks for the whiskey. Take the time, Danny. Think, somewhere in your memory might well be the image of her making that arrangement to meet with her killer in the Bronx."

He didn't see me out. When I stepped out of the heavy door into the street, the dusk was quickening and the birds were raising hell in the trees, getting ready for the night.

I climbed behind the wheel of the Jag and sat staring down the street. I was seeing his face, all his expressions of astonishment and disbelief and distress. He was a good actor. Had any of it been real? Had I learned anything?

I decided I had. I had learned that the night Kate was beaten and stabbed to death, either Danny Santos or Henry Silva could have done it.

Either or both.

SEVEN

I found Dehan at our desk surrounded by a drift of papers and photographs. She was writing on a graph she had drawn up which seemed to correlate credit and debit card payments and phone calls.

"You turning dinosaur?" I dropped into my chair and pointed at the pile. "I thought you were supposed to do that sort of thing with AI."

She didn't look up, but I saw her smile. "I have this guy who is trying to make me more primitive and primal. Did you know books used to be made of paper and had a smell?"

"Find anything interesting?"

"I don't know. Maybe. How'd it go with Danny Santos?"

I recounted our conversation, and halfway through, she flopped back in her chair, tapping her teeth softly with her pen. When I was done, she asked me, "Do you think he was telling the truth about him and Kate?"

I puffed out my cheeks and thought about the question

for the hundredth time. "It's hard to tell. He seemed convincing, but he's a good actor. He subtly directed suspicion toward Silva by telling me it was inconceivable that Silva and Kate were having an affair, or words to that effect. Was that deliberate or a sincere expression of his opinion? I just don't know. One thing did become very clear, though."

"Their alibis ain't worth shit."

"Either one of them, or both of them, could have slipped out during the party and made it there and back within an hour."

She frowned. "Both of them? You think that's a possibility?"

"As much as any other right now. If we are thinking in terms of Kate blackmailing one of them, they both had a lot to lose. It would make sense for them to collaborate, even if only as far as providing an alibi."

She shifted her gaze to the ceiling and started tapping her chin instead of her teeth with her pen.

"Let me tell you what I am hearing," she said. "I'm hearing that Kate tried to blackmail Henry Silva and Danny Santos by revealing to the media that America's sweethearts had an open relationship, and they killed her and provided each other with alibis, and our problem is finding evidence to prove it."

I nodded. "It is beginning to look that way, simply because there is no other suspect, and there is no other motive. Her life was too closely tied to theirs."

"Yeah, I would agree with you but for one small thing. Now I am going to pull a Stone on you." She took a photograph and tossed it across the desk at me. "What do you notice?"

It was a picture of Kate Hagan lying on the floor of her room in a pool of blood. I scanned the photograph, taking in the closed curtains, the bed, the two bedside tables, the huge, dark stain on the pale blue carpet, the chair in the corner.

I gave my head a small shake. "The beating didn't kill her? She bled out from the stab wounds. I don't know. Give me a clue."

"The bed."

"What about the—"

I stopped dead and looked at it. "It's a king."

"She specifically asked for a king-sized bed and paid extra for it. To me, that says she didn't plan to occupy it on her own."

"Son of a gun. She was having an affair."

"So it was either Danny or Henry Silva, or they are protecting whoever killed her."

"It's hard to see it any other way."

I pulled my cell from my pocket. Dehan spoke without looking up. "What are you doing?"

"I'm going to call Jane. Those three are so much in each other's pockets, whatever two of them were aware of, the third was aware of it too. I want to talk to her about—"

"I already called her."

"Oh, and?"

She started gathering up the papers into a folder. "Right now, she's visiting friends in Oyster Bay. But she asked me to visit her on set tomorrow, on West 57th Street."

"She asked you to *visit* her?"

"Yup."

"Can I come and visit with you?"

"She asked if it could be just us girls. I told her I didn't think so."

"Well, that's a relief."

"Drive me home, Stone. I am tired, and I need you to make dinner while we talk about Kate Hagan. I also need to watch you have a martini while you cook."

"I think I can manage that. Come on, kiddo."

As we walked out, Mo at the desk across the way muttered something about us being nauseating, but we ignored him.

———

WE MANAGED to find a spot to park out front and pushed through the big glass doors into the lobby. I leaned on the desk and smiled at the teeth that were grinning back at me. I showed her my card. "Detectives John Stone and Carmen Dehan, NYPD." Dehan leaned next to me and said, "He's John, and I'm Carmen. We're here to see Jane Morley. She's expecting us."

Her laugh was nothing if not nervous. She glanced at us both as she giggled, like maybe she was missing some subtle woke trap. "I'll let her know you're here. Do make yourselves comfortable."

We took a stroll looking at a multitude of photographs of people who had become famous riding into other people's living rooms on tidal waves of canned laughter.

Dehan stood close by my side. "The only way to avoid the Swamp of Woke," she said, providing the words with capitalized initials, "is to acquire antigravity through not giving a damn."

I smiled as I moved on to a picture of Larry Rhodes. "So at what age did you become weightless, Dehan? Two? Three?"

"Before that, Stone," she said with no trace of humor. She made a sliding motion with her right hand. "I just *floated* out of my mama's womb. That midwife had to get a ladder just to drag me down from the ceiling. Did I care?"

"Did you care?"

"Nope."

A voice echoed across the lobby. "Carmen?"

We both turned.

He must have been in his mid-twenties, though he had very skillfully made himself look twelve years younger. His skin looked like oiled tissue paper in which all and any hair follicles had been stillborn. The hair on his head was pointed and a brilliant cream white, like the ice cream on top of a cone. When he spoke, he had a habit of placing his knees and his hands together, like he was about to dive into a pool.

I smiled absently. Dehan did not look amused. She pulled her badge from her pocket and held it up for him to see. "*Detective* Carmen Dehan, New York Police Department. This is my partner, *Detective* John Stone. We are here to see Jane Morley."

His very pale cheeks took on the same color as his very pink lips. "Of course. I am Dennis," he said.

"Maybe you thought we were here for a tour of the studios, Dennis."

He gave a surprisingly guttural laugh with lots of teeth. "Jane is just shooting. If you'll follow me."

We followed him down a long corridor which was probably big enough to fit a sixteen-wheeler and a couple of cars, around a dogleg and through large double doors onto a soundstage. It was all dark except for a glowing area against the far wall. The doors closed behind us, and a voice shouted, "*Okay, silence please, aaand action!*"

Eight or ten feet in front of me, there were several people sitting in folding canvas chairs. There were a couple of cameras, one on my right and one over on my left. Directly ahead of me was a generic, comfortable, middle class living room. A flight of stairs rose into shadow. Jane was sitting cross-legged on the sofa. She turned a page, and feet were heard trotting down the stairs. Danny appeared, fixing the knot on his tie. He took a couple of steps and started doing up his cuffs.

Jane said, "A security guard was injured and four men were shot dead in a bank raid in Houston yesterday."

"No kidding. Did the robbers get away?"

"They were the robbers."

"So if they shot the security guard, who shot them?"

"Everybody else in the bank. This is Texas we're talking about." Canned laughter broke out. "There was an eighty-year-old grandmother who scored a headshot, and the mayor is awarding her a medal." More laughter.

Danny turned and gestured at her. "See? And you wanted to badooble blabba dubble Oh my God! Is it me? Am I becoming senile? Or is it this shit script!"

An anonymous voice shouted, "Cut! Okay, take a break! Danny, go over your lines, will you?"

The lights came on, and suddenly, there was movement all around us. On the stage, we saw Dennis preparing to dive beside Jane. She nodded and stood. The crowds parted as she approached, and within ten feet from us, she switched on her smile. "Carmen! How lovely to see you!" Her eyes froze over as she turned to me. "John, I didn't realize you were coming. Would you like to talk to Danny while Carmen and I do girly stuff?"

I didn't return the frozen smile. "No. We're working, Jane, and Detective Dehan has no time for girly stuff. Neither have I, for that matter. Is there somewhere quiet we can talk?"

She turned to Dehan, rolled her eyes, and sighed. "Follow me."

We crossed the crowded floor. That disembodied voice called, "Jane?"

She turned back. "Gimme ten, ten minutes. I'll be right back."

I thought about telling him we'd be as long as it took but decided against it and followed her through a side door to a narrow passage and eventually to a small dressing room. She went in ahead, Dehan followed, and I closed the door after me.

She smiled at Dehan, turned a cold face to me, and opened her mouth. I was running out of patience, so I cut her dead.

"Can it, Jane. This is a murder investigation. One of your closest friends was beaten half to death and then stabbed, remember? This is not a scripted role in a movie, and we are not playing games. This is not a social call, and I am not gate-crashing on your and Detective Dehan's girly party. We are investigating the murder of Kate Hagan. Do we understand each other?"

You could have saved polar bears with her face. "Perfectly."

Jane had sat at her dressing table, and Dehan had taken the only other chair. So I leaned against the door and crossed my arms.

"Here's the thing, Jane. You, Henry Silva, and Danny Santos were all each other's alibis. You went to the gala together, then you went to the party together. You were seen arrive by hundreds of people, you were seen going to the party with Jack Roch by dozens, but the fact is that while you were there, at both events, the only people who had eyes on you all of the time were you three."

"So?"

"Well, now it turns out that in fact you and Henry Silva went off on your own, and Danny hardly saw you all night. Which means that you didn't see him, either. But your relationship with Silva was over by then, so how long were you both in each other's company?"

I paused. Her eyes were bright and frightened. I pressed her.

"I don't need to tell you, Jane, that conspiring to protect a murderer can carry very serious time. And let me tell you that you are not designed to survive in prison. If Silva or your husband had anything going with Kate, we need to know about it now."

Her lips were trembling.

"We know you didn't have sight of your husband all night. We know you hardly saw him after you arrived. What we need to know is whether you had sight of Silva all night."

She swallowed hard. Dehan spoke, and her voice was gentle and understanding.

"Jane, we know that Kate booked the room at the hotel,

and we know that she insisted on a king bed. We know she was meeting someone there."

Her voice was a rasp. "It could have been anyone."

I asked her, "Could it? Think about it. In the two weeks leading up to Jack Roch's gala, how long was Kate out of your sight at any one time?" I gave her a moment. She didn't answer. "How long was she out of the house if she wasn't with you? How many men did she talk to in those two weeks?" I paused again. Her eyes were wild, looking this way and that into the corners of the room, like she was searching for the answers to my questions.

"I'll tell you how many, Jane. Two. And you know it. She saw Danny, and she saw Henry Silva. And neither of them has an alibi for that night. Both or either of them could have slipped away and returned without anyone noticing."

"Jesus Christ, are you out of your mind? Kate having an affair with..." She trailed off, and her face said suddenly it wasn't looking so impossible. "I can't. It's just not..."

I growled. "I am not interested in your opinion, Jane. I want to know if you had eyes on Silva all night or if you lost sight of him."

She stared at me a long while with resentment in her eyes. "I lost sight of them both," she said eventually. "I was with Simon."

"Who is Simon?"

"He was a young aspiring actor. He was fun, and he took me out of myself..."

"Save it for the confessional. How long were you with him?"

"All night, from shortly after we arrived. Will you need to talk to him? He was married, still is."

I sighed. "I don't know. We won't if we don't need to. What's his surname?"

"Do you need to? Can't you just take it from me?"

"What's his surname, Jane?"

"I don't remember."

Dehan stood and hunkered down in front of her. She took both her hands and held them gently, looking up into her face. "Jane, Stone comes on strong sometimes, as you well know, but he's a good man and a decent human being. But the law is the law, and law enforcement is a machine that when it gets going is ruthless and relentless. If you tell us this guy's name, we'll go talk to him if we have to, and we'll be discreet. But if you make us look for him, the machine will kick in, and we will leave no skeleton unturned until we find him. And there will be no way of hiding it. Work with us, and we will do our best to be discreet."

Jane stared for a long moment into Dehan's face, then her eyes shifted up to me. "You could learn something from this woman, John."

"Tell me something I didn't know, like Simon's surname."

"Browne."

"Simon Browne? Are you serious?"

"Browne with an E. That's his name. It happens to be a very common name. That's why he put an E on the end."

"And where can we find him?"

She smiled at Dehan and gave her hands a squeeze. She gave her the answer. "I honestly don't know. I'll have to make some inquiries, and I shall call you later today." She glanced at me, then spoke to Dehan again. "Now I really must get back to the set. We run a very tight ship, and every minute wasted is a thousand bucks down the shoot." She stood. "You'll see yourselves out, won't you?"

She left the room without looking at me. Dehan was still hunkered down with her elbows on her knees, frowning at my shoes.

"Why are you so hard on her, Stone?"

"Am I?"

"Pretty hard. She's not a suspect."

"Then why is she lying to us?"

She sighed. "Because she is trying to protect somebody." She gave her mouth a little twist and studied me from down on the floor. "Are you jealous? Is that why you're being so hard? Are you jealous of the guy she's protecting?"

"Not even a little. I'm just being a cop." I stepped over and held out my hand. "Come on, Little Grasshopper. We have work to do."

She took my hand, and I pulled her up. For a second, we were very close, and she slipped her arms around me and buried her face in my neck. "Sometimes life sucks, Stone."

All I could do was kiss the top of her head and tell her I knew.

EIGHT

We found our way back to the sound stage. Jane was sitting on the sofa again, legs crossed and leafing through a magazine. Danny was standing with a towel around his neck while somebody did something to his face. Everybody else was standing at ease in the half-shadows watching the characters on the brightly lit stage.

I paused a moment as Dehan reached for the door. There was something about the scene I could not put into words. Dehan paused to wait, watching me. I was barely aware of her. I was very aware of the fact that everything was in shadow except the stage, where the characters were. Dehan came back to me. I heard her whisper, "What?"

I spoke aloud, but I was asking myself more than her. "Is that congruous or incongruous?"

She frowned, but before she could answer, another voice broke in.

"You the detectives?"

I turned and saw a woman leaning on a spotlight. She

had a baseball cap on backwards over short blond hair. Her features were regular and attractive, but her eyes were challenging and ironic, which was oddly off-putting. She had a medium to short and vaguely shapeless figure under a roll-neck sweater and dungarees.

"Yeah, I'm Stone, this is my partner, Detective Dehan. You work here?"

She gave Dehan a cursory glance and turned her attention back to me. "Bella, Bella Milano, I'm the gaffer. I take care of the lights and the electrics. That's the theory. Actually I bin here twenty-five years, since I was fifteen, and I take care of everything. You're here about Kate, right?"

I arched an eyebrow, and she laughed. "You don't become indispensable without listening to gossip, Stone."

"You knew Kate?"

"Yeah, I knew Kate. She was a doll. Everybody loved Kate." She paused, watching me with humorous eyes. "They loved her because she was sweet and kind and helpful under pressure, but mainly because she kept Jane on task. Jane is adorable, we all adore her, but she can be a pain in the ass when she is frustrated or things don't go her way. You know what I'm saying? But Kate knew exactly how to handle her, and she needed Kate like she needed air." She turned to watch Jane on the sofa. "When Kate died, Jane went to pieces. Some people thought she was finished. But she's a tough cookie, and she came back."

Dehan said, "Who keeps her on task now?"

Bella swiveled her eyes and gave Dehan a once-over. "It's a joint effort."

"You said after twenty-five years, you took care of everything. Do you take care of Jane too?"

Bella smiled on the right side of her face and looked away. "Yeah, sometimes. She's known me a long time, and she trusts me. She knows I don't take no drama queen shit. So sometimes I have to go talk to her and bring her back on set—or to the studio. Depends how high up the diva scale she's climbed."

I asked, "Who was Kate getting close to back then?"

She shook her head. "Kate never got close to nobody except Jane."

"How about Danny? Was she close to him?"

She shrugged, pulled down the corners of her mouth, and looked away. "I don't know what goes on behind closed doors, Stone. On set, he was just her husband."

Dehan folded her arms. "You just told us essential people listen to gossip. What you meant was, people become essential when they know what's going on. Now I am going to tell you something, Bella. During the two weeks prior to her death, perhaps longer, Kate became close to somebody. So close that they became sexually intimate. Now you and I both know that when a change like that happens in somebody's life, the people close to them notice. With somebody like Kate, who was tied to Jane and Danny practically twenty-four hours a day, that change is going to be a hundred times more noticeable. But you are telling us you, Captain Essential, didn't see it?"

Bella took a deep breath. On the stage, people were being called to their stations.

"Let me give it some thought. It was a long time ago. Gimme a card. I'll be in touch if I think of anything."

I gave her a card. Her hand when she took it was surprisingly delicate. I thanked her, and we pushed out of the studio.

Out on West 57th, the cool sunlight had become patchy under fluffy clouds that were getting fat and showing gray patches that promised rain. I walked around the hood to the driver's side, but Dehan laid her forearms on the roof and rested her chin on her arms. I smiled at her.

"What?"

"Nobody noticed. *Nobody* noticed. You notice—one notices, as you would say—because the besotted person's behavior changes."

"The besotted person?"

"Uh-huh. They start doing things they didn't do before, gazing into the middle distance, saying things and making observations or comments that are uncharacteristic, checking their cell phones every thirty seconds. You know the stuff."

"Yup."

"Someone like Kate, who is on top of Jane's life at every moment, who knows exactly what Jane has done, is doing and is going to do, preempts everything and does it well enough A, to become essential and B, to be constantly praised by everyone *including* Jane. That means one thing, Stone."

I leaned on the roof, facing her. "Tell me."

"It means that every damned minute of her day was devoted to Jane, and, to a lesser degree, to Danny. However much their private lives may be separate, this couple lives mainly public lives. Their private lives are private *moments*, when they get a chance. So Kate managed Jane's life, and to some extent Danny's, because the two were entwined. And that took up *all of her waking hours*. Do you agree?"

"I agree."

"But nobody noticed—and more to the point, Stone, considering we are dealing with a bunch of narcissists, nobody *complained*, that she was suddenly gazing into the middle distance and checking her cell instead of arranging an interview with *Hello* magazine or an appointment with a hair stylist or a beautician. What is more, her cell phone records don't show calls coming in or going out every thirty seconds. And she is not suddenly in contact with a new cell phone." She gave her head an exasperated shake. "I hate to say it, but I think these bozos are telling the truth. They didn't notice a change in her or her behavior because there wasn't one."

I took a deep breath and sighed. Then I climbed in the car and slammed the door, and she got in beside me.

"I think you're right," I said. "Which leads us irresistibly —" I stopped dead, then started again. "She booked a hotel room and insisted on a king bed. So we deduce from that that she was in a sexually intimate relationship. That's a pretty safe assumption. And that fact, together with the fact that nobody seemed to notice a corresponding change in her behavior, leads us *irresistibly* to…" I paused, aware my mind was racing on ahead of me, and Dehan finished for me.

"She was screwing someone she was already in close contact with. That's why there was no change in her behavior. Because she was already seeing that person and talking to them on a regular basis. The only guys who fit that bill are Henry Silva and Danny Santos. So she was screwing one of them. We just need to prove it." I drew breath, but she went on. "We don't need to talk to Simon Toyboy Browne with an E. And Jane doesn't need an alibi, Stone. We need to talk to the hookers Roch arranged for Danny—if they exist. And we need to take Silva apart because neither Jane nor Danny can vouch for where he was anymore."

I thought for a moment, nodded, and turned the key in the ignition.

"Agreed. Now we just need to find two high-class hookers who were at a party thrown by a guy who paid several thousand dollars for total discretion ten years ago."

"Hey, focus on the negative, why don't you?"

As I moved east down West 57th, she pulled her cell from her pocket and began to dial. She put it on speaker. After a couple of rings, a woman's voice said, "Gold and Silva Talent Agency. How may I help you?"

"This is Detective Carmen Dehan of the New York Police Department. I need to speak to Henry Silva."

"Mr. Silva has gone to the country. I'm afraid he won't be back until next week."

"Okay, thanks."

She hung up, and I handed her Silva's card. She dialed and put it on speaker.

"Hello, who is this?"

"Mr. Silva, this is Detective Dehan."

"Oh, look, I'm sorry. I'm not in town right now. I won't be back till—"

"I know, Mr. Silva. There has been a development in the case, and we need to talk to you now. It can't wait till next week."

There was a note of disbelief in his voice. He gave a small

laugh. "Well, I can't very well drive back to the city. I have commitments."

Dehan laughed. "Well, don't let a small thing like murder cause you any inconvenience, sir. We'll come to you."

He sighed. "Look—"

I cut in. "If that's not convenient, I can send a car for you. As Detective Dehan said, there has been a development in the case, and we need to clear up a few details with you. I'll remind them to keep their sirens switched off."

"Are you threatening me, Detective Stone?"

"I'm not sure, Mr. Silva. Maybe I am just warning you that this might be a little more serious than you assume. It would be a really good idea, sir, if you made time to see us this afternoon."

"I see. Fine, will four p.m. suit you? How long is this likely to take?"

Dehan answered. "Well, sir, if you cooperate with us and don't tell us any more lies, it shouldn't take more than ten or fifteen minutes."

"Lies? I—"

"Save it for later, sir. If you could just give us the address."

He gave us an address on Palisade Avenue in Riverdale, a couple of miles south of Yonkers. Then he added, "I have to tell you, Detectives, I object strongly to the attitude you have taken with me, and I shall let your superiors know."

"The chief will be very glad to hear from you, sir. We'll see you at four p.m. Thank you for seeing us."

She hung up, then looked at me. "He's the guy."

"What about Bobby Newport? Are we just dropping him?"

She nodded. "He's not the guy, Stone. You know it. You were the first to say it. Jane was with Simon. We have no reason to disbelieve that. Danny was with Roch's hookers. We have to confirm that, and we will. That leaves Silva, and he has given me the creeps from the start."

"'He's the guy, Your Honor, he gives me the creeps.' 'Not another word, Detective Dehan, I shall instruct the jury to find the accused guilty, and not only that, we shall reinstate the death penalty. That'll show the cad, what!'"

"I wish I could say that was funny, Stone. I really do. He's the guy. We have to prove it, but he's the guy, and you know it."

Back at the station, while Dehan went to get coffee, I called Bernie, my contact at the Bureau.

"Stone, how's it hangin', man?"

"Perpendicular to the floor. How are you, Bernie?"

"Hangin' in there. What can I do for you?"

"I'm not sure you can do anything, but I've got to ask. I need to track down two high-class hookers."

I waited for him to stop laughing. When he'd reached the stage of sighing and wiping his eyes, he said, "In New York? Two high-class hookers in New York? You heard about the haystack, right?"

"Yeah, I know, but hear me out. These are *real* high class. We are talking about Jack Roch hiring these two girls for Danny Santos."

"America's sweethearts Danny Santos?"

"Right. Danny Santos, Jane Morley, and their agent, Henry Silva, get invited to galas that only somebody who is somebody gets invited to. And then, afterwards, the very select among the somebodies get invited to the private do in the penthouse. These three are among the very select."

"Okay, I hear you."

"So I have a gala in honor of Jack Roch's birthday. After the gala, Jane Morley, Danny Santos, and Henry Silva get invited to the private party at the penthouse. Now the working theory at the moment is that while everybody was out of their skulls on booze and cocaine, Danny hopped over to the Bronx, murdered the victim, and sped back to the penthouse in Manhattan in time for a last snort and a drive home at dawn in his Rolls Royce. But his alibi, for what it's worth, is that Jack Roch had fixed him up with two hookers for the night."

"And you want to know if those hookers can be found."

"I do."

He sighed, but it wasn't the heavy sigh I was expecting. "At that level, it's not as hard as you might think. We have friendly informers and people on the payroll at that level. But if I can get you anything, it won't be anything you can use in court. You understand that?"

"Sure. Just knowing would be a help."

"You said it was Jack Roch's birthday? When was that?"

I winced. "Tenth August, ten years ago."

"*Ten years ago?*"

"Hey! I do cold cases, remember? By the way, how was the twenty-year-old Bushmills I sent you for *your* birthday?"

He groaned. "Superb. Okay, Stone, I will make discreet inquiries. The salons available for that class of gig are a small handful. Seeing as they are big names like Roch and Danny Santos, we might just get lucky, but don't count on it. And like I said, you won't be able to use this in court. It is *strictly* off the record."

"Okay, you're a pal."

"Christmas is just around the corner, pal. I'll be watching my mailbox."

I laughed, and we hung up with promises to catch up soon.

Dehan appeared with coffee and placed one in front of me. I said, "I don't want you to come."

She sipped and watched me but didn't say anything.

"If you're right and he's the guy, it's too risky. We agreed on this already, right?"

She nodded. "So if I don't go, who'll have your back?"

"I'll be armed. I worked without a partner for a long time before you came along. I'll be fine."

"I could come and wait in the car."

"Last time we did that, you showed up at my elbow as he opened the door." I smiled at her. "I'm not asking."

She sighed. "Okay."

NINE

Henry Silva's house in Riverdale was tucked away on a little road a stone's throw from the Hudson that was almost completely concealed by a superabundance of trees. The house was large though unassuming, with two stories and windows at ground level that suggested a cellar. There was a newer wing on the left that might have been from the '50s and an older wing that might have been a hundred years old or a little more.

There was a short drive paved in red and brown cobbles that was occupied by a dark blue Mercedes limousine and a cream Honda Accord. A large oak door stood in an older wing of the house. The newer extension was to the left, painted in white with large plate glass windows on the upper floor. I climbed from the Jag and stood looking up, telling myself the plate glass must afford a spectacular view of the river across the treetops in Riverdale Park.

As I moved toward the door, I noticed absently that one of those windows was open a few inches, and I could just make out the strains of Maria Callas singing "J'ai Perdu mon Eurydice" from Gluck's *Orphée et Eurydice*.

I reached the door, and as I pressed the bell, I realized the door was pulled to, but not closed. I pushed it gently with my finger, and it swung silently open. The music became slightly louder.

"Mr. Silva? It's Detective Stone from the NYPD."

The only sound that came back to me was the distant echo of my own voice. I stepped over the threshold into a broad hall of irregular shape. A flight of stairs rose into shadows immediately on my right. At the top, I could see a landing but not much more. The music now seemed to be coming from up there.

Ahead of me, the hall made a dogleg into a nook on the right, in the crook of the stairs, where I could see a couple of coats hanging from a row of hooks on the wall. There were rubber boots on the floor and a couple of umbrellas and walking sticks in a large earthenware vase. Directly opposite me was what I took to be a door into the living room. It was flanked by strips of stained glass that looked like genuine art deco. I called again but was answered only by Maria Callas.

I took the first step up toward the landing, and as I took the second, I heard the living room door crash open behind me. I turned my head but only caught a dark blur. Then there was a crashing, piercing pain in my head, followed instantly by blackness.

I had no idea at the time how long I was out. I later discovered it was only a couple of minutes. All I knew was that I was aware of a feeling of nausea and throbbing pain that seemed to permeate all of me to drag me back out of the blackness. Gradually, I became aware that I was lying face down on the stairs, with the carpet and the edge of the stairs biting into my cheek. I forced myself onto one elbow, and the house rocked, first away from me and then back up to meet me. I steadied myself and felt the back of my head. There was no blood, but it hurt. I quietly congratulated myself on telling Dehan to stay at the station, carefully got myself into a kneeling position, then propped myself against the banisters and managed to stand. The earth moved for all the wrong reasons but settled after a moment, and I felt under my arm for my weapon. It was still there. Whoever had slugged me had been in a hurry, but their intention had been to get away, not to cause me serious harm. I began to climb.

It crossed my mind it might have been Silva, but he was a strong guy, and I would have expected the blow to be harder. On the other hand, it had been a glancing blow as he made for the door. The jury would have to stay out on that one for now.

On the landing, it dawned on me that Maria Callas was still singing the same song. That didn't make a lot of sense. The song should have ended by now. It was coming from a half-open door at the end of a long corridor. The corridor was dark, but an angle of bright light lay across the floor.

I called out again, "Mr. Silva? It's Detective Stone. Are you there?"

There was no reply. I prefer not to use a weapon if I can avoid it, but I reached under my arm and pulled the Sig from my holster. Then I moved down the corridor toward the half-open door. The music grew louder. I didn't call Silva again. I knew he wasn't going to answer. I pushed the door gently with my foot, keeping the Sig held out in front of me.

The music was loud. Maria Callas' beautiful, plaintive voice cried that she had lost her Eurydice. But it was not Eurydice sitting in the chair at the large, oak desk facing the door. It was Silva. He had a thick electrical cable draped around his shoulders, a deep purple bruise around his neck, and bloody claw marks down his throat. His face was a ghastly purple gray and grotesquely swollen. His eyes were bulging, goggling at me but seeing nothing.

I called it in, then called Dehan.

"I arrived five minutes too late. Silva has been murdered."

She was quiet a moment. Then, "That complicates things, huh? You okay?"

"I'm better than Silva. I got a bump on the head, he got strangled with electrical wire. His killer was still here when I arrived. He snuck up on me when I was going up the stairs."

"You called it in?"

"Yeah, Frank and Joe are on their way."

"Me too. We need to think about this. I mean, why? Right? And who knew you were going to talk to him?"

"Mm-hmm. Maybe he called somebody. Get here. There are things I want you to see. And hear."

"I'm on my way."

She arrived half an hour later with a couple of squad cars. While the uniforms set about taping off the area, I took her upstairs to the den. On the way up, I told her what had happened.

"I must have arrived just a couple of minutes too late. The killer was still here. The door was open, I came in, and as I was taking the first steps, he rushed me from behind and clubbed me."

She stopped. We were halfway up, but she went back down a couple of steps to look at the hall.

"Why were you going upstairs? He came out of the living room?" She pointed at the art deco doors. I nodded. "I could hear music coming from upstairs.'

She pointed up through the ceiling. "That same music?"

"Maria Callas singing 'J'ai Perdu mon Eurydice.' It's from an opera by Christoph Willibald Gluck called *Orphée et Eurydice*."

"And it's still going? What is it, one of those German operas that goes on for days? How long is this song?"

"No, but that is kind of my point. The song is on a loop. I could hear it when I arrived, and I could still hear it when I came around. And almost an hour later, it's still going. It means something, but I have no idea what."

She stared at me a moment and made a 'Huh!' noise, then we went up to the den.

We stood in the doorway, and Silva goggled at us from his chair.

"That looks like electrical cable around his neck."

I gave a couple of slow nods. "Several things stand out. First is that Silva was a strong, fit guy. It would not have been easy to strangle him like that. He would have fought and struggled. And yet..."

I trailed off, and she took over. "And yet the desk is undisturbed, and he is sitting in his chair like he just sat there and let it happen.'

"The only sign of struggle"—I took a couple of steps closer and pointed—"are those claw marks on his neck. He sat there and tore the skin from his throat trying to release the cable, but he didn't try to stand or get away from his assailant."

"Right." She crossed her arms and leaned on the jamb. "And he was quite happy to let his killer get behind him while he sat at his desk."

Outside, I could hear Frank's old station wagon pulling up and the crime scene van pulling into the drive behind my Jaguar.

"I think," I said, "Joe is going to find there are no signs of a break-in. He knew the guy. This is going to be like Kate's death in that the killing was executed by somebody who was close to their inner circle. He let him in, they came up, chatted. The killer was pacing the room while Silva sat at his desk. They were discussing work or whatever, and this guy wandered behind him, put the cable around his neck, and killed him."

She winced. "That all makes sense to me up to that last bit. There is nothing behind his desk except a wall with a couple of awards. That would be real unnatural, wandering behind him like that."

"I agree, and yet." I shook my head, trying to visualize the unnatural scene. "He was strangled from behind, and he sat there and took it."

The sound of tramping feet came to me from the stairs. I turned as Frank and Joe entered the room, Joe dressed like an extra from ET. Frank gave us the kind of greeting you reserve for a complete stranger and crossed the room to the body. Joe followed him.

"Is that electrical cable around his shoulders?"

Frank nodded. "Bag it please. It's in my way."

I said, "It's consistent with the murder weapon, right?"

He didn't look at me. "When I have determined cause of death, I will be able to answer that question, John."

Dehan chuckled, and I sighed. "It's consistent with what made that bruise around his neck, where he tore at his throat like he was being strangled."

"That may well be the case, John. I will tell you when I have determined cause of death. Is there anything else before you leave and let me get on with my job?"

"Yes. I want to know why he sat there without moving anything except his arms. He was violently distressed, enough to tear the skin from his throat, but he didn't stand or thrash, or knock the chair over. Nothing. So was he drugged, was he tased?"

"All right. Goodbye."

Dehan spoke to Joe as he was dropping the cable into a plastic evidence bag. "I'm thinking it can't be easy to strangle a guy like Silva with a cable like that. Piano wire would have been easier. He had to grip it real hard, right? So unless he wore gloves, there has to be bits of the killer's hands on that cable, at the ends where he gripped it."

Joe nodded. "Very possible. Unless, like you said, he wore gloves."

I approached him. "Two more things, Joe: When I entered the house, the killer was waiting for me behind the living room door. As I climbed the stairs, he rushed out and hit me. There might be traces there."

"K."

"And the music. It was playing when I arrived, and it's on some kind of a loop. It has to be on a pen drive or something of the sort. Two gets you twenty the killer put it on for some reason."

Frank cleared his throat. "Maria Callas, beautiful but overrated. And this is a man's song. Orpheus sings it when Eurydice dies. 'What shall I do without Eurydice? I have lost my Eurydice.'" He glanced up at us from Silva's neck. "You're still here? You're not in a hurry for the results? You want to stop and chat a while?"

We left them to it and went downstairs. There was a guy in a plastic suit hunkered down inspecting the lock. I paused beside him.

"It wasn't forced, was it?"

"Nope. Ain't nobody done nothin' to this lock 'sept open and close the door."

We had a wander around the house, bagged a few things like his cell, then went out and sat on the hood of the Jag while they wheeled the gurney in to collect the body. I noticed the car that was missing was the Honda and cursed myself for not making a mental note of the model and license plate. I pointed at the empty space beside the Merc.

"There was a Honda parked there. I didn't make a note."

She screwed up her face. "Stone, our pool of suspects is too small. I mean"—she gestured with both hands at the space I had pointed at—"let's imagine for a moment that it was actually the killer's car, not rented, borrowed, or stolen. Imagine you are one of those people who has a photographic memory, and you take a snap of the two cars. All you need to do now is check if it's...let me think..."—she made an elaborate show of thinking—"oh, Danny's. Because that *is* our pool of suspects. Okay, maybe it's Bob Newport's, but that is very unlikely. So our pool of suspects is one person."

I felt the back of my head and winced while I considered that she was right. She went on.

"The car was rented or stolen. There is only one person more aware than we are of how small our suspect pool is, and that's the killer." She shook her head. "Stone, I was *so* sure he was the guy."

I thought about that for a moment as they wheeled the gurney into the house.

"What makes you assume he wasn't?"

She stared at me for a moment. Then stared at the disappearing gurney.

All she said was, "Huh…!"

TEN

We spent the evening and most of the next morning securing and examining Silva's phone records and talking to Mrs. Hastings, his secretary, on the telephone about what plans and appointments he'd had for that week. She was extremely upset, trying hard not to show it and failing spectacularly at regular intervals.

"He canceled all his appointments for this week after you came and started harassing him. He was such a good man. How could anyone…" A few moments of silence was broken by an impressive groan followed by, "I'm sorry. I just can't. But I must. He would expect us all to soldier on. He was such a good man. He canceled everything for this week after Ms. Hagan's murder resurfaced. Why they couldn't leave well enough alone…"

I interrupted while she groaned again and asked, "What was the purpose of taking the week off? What did he intend to do during that week?"

She sobbed, "I don't know. He was such a *good* man."

"Mrs. Hastings, you want his killer caught and punished, don't you?"

She made a damp noise that sounded affirmative. I pressed her.

"It may well be the same person who killed Kate Hagan ten years ago, and we don't know who will be next. So we really need you to focus on what he told you and any small clue it might throw up about what his intentions were for this week."

There was a small sound of damp thinking. I pressed on.

"We know why he took the week off—because Kate Hagan's case had resurfaced. But what his intentions were for that week we don't know. Whatever they were might well have led to his murder. So it is very important for us to have any clues you can give about what he intended to do this week."

A damp "Um..." then, "He said, he said he needed time to take care of some personal business. I asked if it was anything I could help with, but he said no, it was..."—she faltered—"it was best I didn't get involved." She started wailing again. "He was such a noble, honorable man!"

We continued for another five minutes or so, but she didn't have any more, and eventually I hung up. I'd had her on speaker, and now Dehan and I sat and stared at each other. She was the first to speak.

"He either knew or suspected who killed Kate. Our taking the case made him take action. He contacted the person he suspected, and they killed him."

I grunted.

She said, "What?"

"That's probably true."

"But you're not convinced." Before I could reply, she went on. "You said yesterday maybe Silva was the guy, and the guy who killed him wasn't the guy. How does that work? Explain that to me."

"I can't. I don't know. I can't get a handle on this."

"Great. So you were just trying to confuse me."

"No. I was thinking aloud. Okay, just for a moment, imagine Danny Santos was in love with Kate, or they were having an affair, and now, somehow, maybe because of our investigation, he realizes that it was in fact Silva who killed her." It was her turn to grunt. "It's like you said, Dehan. There is a tiny pool of suspects. This should be cut and dried. But it ain't. I can't get a handle on it."

She pinched her lower lip and spoke with it pinched. "You still like Danny for it?"

I shrugged. "I don't like anybody for it!"

She was about to answer when my phone rang. I looked at the screen and answered, "Bernie. You got something for me?"

"Maybe, but like I told you already, this is totally unofficial, and you cannot use it."

"I understand."

"I'm not sure you do. You can't draw data about a swamp without getting your sensors dirty, am I right?"

"I guess so, Bernie."

"Sometimes a person, or a putative agency, could theoretically wind up building such a vast structure of dirty sensors that a careless move by some, say, investigator could wind up pulling the whole damn edifice down and causing a lot of damage to the investigators. And let me tell you that some of those sensors go a long way up."

"I understand you, Bernie. I am not in Vice. I just want to know if anybody was with my guy that night."

"Okay, I am sticking my neck out for you here, Stone, because I trust you. Don't go and let me down now, okay?"

"I won't let you down, Bernie. I appreciate the favor. I owe you."

"Okay, so I don't know a damn thing about any of this, but a contact from the friend of a friend's cousin says that it might be useful for you to talk to Katherine Parr. I have Whatsapped you her telephone number, and I would be grateful if you deleted it as soon as you have memorized it. Her address is on the Upper West Side, as you would expect from a couple of very talented actresses. She has a penthouse at 116 Riverside Drive. My friend's friend's cousin says that if you call, she'll see you. But Stone, be discreet and diplomatic, and don't take Carmen."

"I wasn't planning to."

"They'll either hate her and kick you out or they'll love her and offer her a job."

"That's funny," I said with a total absence of humor in my voice, though Dehan was laughing in her chair.

"Not really, John. These women are a lot more powerful than you might think. I'm serious; keep Carmen away from them."

"I hear you. Thanks, Bernie."

I hung up.

"You weren't planning to take me?"

"Of course not. They'd take one look at you and clam up."

"Why?"

"They'd assume you were Vice. You have Vice written all over you."

She actually gasped and gaped. "That is so sexist! Stone! That is so inappropriate."

I wagged a finger at her. "Inappropriate is a pregnant, married woman hanging around high-class whorehouses when she should be at home preparing dinner."

Mo, across the way, laid down his pen and turned to frown at me, and I swear there was reverence in his eyes.

Dehan screwed up a piece of paper and threw it at me without much commitment.

"Fine, Mr. Neanderthal, but I ain't making dinner. You can take me out after you've had a cold shower. Meantime, I am going to follow a few hunches regarding electric cables."

I stood. "Foolish child. I'll call you when I'm done."

I MANAGED to find a parking space on West 83rd and walked the hundred yards to the apartment block, which faced the gardens that run along the banks of the Hudson. There was a doorman in a uniform at the door. His mouth asked if he could help me, but his eyes told me he wondered whom I thought I was.

I said, "I don't know. I'm here to see Ms. Katherine Parr."

His left eyebrow rose an eighth of an inch, and he produced the ghost of a smile which, when it was alive, might have been contempt.

"Of course, sir." He opened the door and pointed a white-gloved finger. "The elevator on the right, all the way to the top. Apartment B."

The elevator was all walnut with a very shiny mirror and cute lamps with small green shades. It took me to the top floor, but if there hadn't been a screen showing me the numbers, I'd have thought we were not moving. On the seventeenth floor, the doors hissed open with a sigh I'd have sworn was sheer pleasure, and I stepped out into a short corridor with dark, wood paneled walls with those little brass lamps with green shades and a sage green carpet. The door to Apartment B was also walnut.

It opened after I had rung twice, and a guy who looked like a sumo wrestler in a white jacket opened the door. I smiled at him, but I might as well have smiled at the north face of the Eiger.

"I have an appointment to see Ms. Katherine Parr. My name is—"

"No name. You come."

He turned his back on me and walked away. His legs were like small redwood trees but were oddly knock-kneed, which made him both terrifying and ridiculous at the same time.

The door closed behind me of its own accord, and I followed him through a large, elegant entrance hall and down a corridor that smelled of the kind of incense you believe is an aphrodisiac when you're eighteen but isn't to another door. He rapped on it and opened it.

"Go in."

I wasn't going to argue. I stepped into a large drawing room that overlooked the park. It was decorated and furnished in a minimalist Scandinavian style, and large, sliding glass doors gave on to an ample terrace. Those doors were closed, but between me and them, there was an extremely beautiful woman sitting on a large calico sofa beside an open fire. She was watching me. I watched her back for a moment. Her hair was auburn and on the wild side of curly. Her eyes were a deep green, and her skin was pale. She was in her late twenties or early thirties. She was dressed in a sweatshirt and leggings, but she made them look like an Armani evening dress.

"Ms. Katherine Parr?"

"Clearly that isn't my name any more than you are Henry Tudor. Nor do I want to know your name. You are not here, and I have never spoken to you. I hope that is clear."

"Very. May I sit, or do I have to do this interview standing?"

"Before you sit, I want you to understand that I am recording this interview, and that you passed through a sensor at the door which would have picked up a wire if you were wearing one. If I ever use this recording, it will be because you have screwed up my business, and my life won't be worth living. My business is built on foundations of trust, and, if you'll excuse the taxing of the metaphor, the protective walls and the ceiling are provided by people who govern states and sit in Congress, amongst other places. It would be very bad for you and for me if anybody ever heard about this conversation. Are we one hundred percent clear?"

"You have made yourself very clear. May I sit down now?"

She gestured to a large calico armchair opposite her on the other side of the fireplace. I sat. She watched me and waited. Her eyes were beautiful but hostile.

"Katherine, it has been made very clear to me by the

person who put us in touch that it is very much in everybody's interest"—I paused a moment and held her eye to make sure she knew I was referring to the Bureau—"that you are not professionally embarrassed. I have no desire—or need—to inconvenience you. Much less do I want to compromise the relationship I have with my friend, as I am sure you can imagine. So can we please take it as read that I am not here to cause you trouble? I know, I have been told very clearly, that whatever information I get here, I cannot reveal the source."

She gave a simple nod. "What do you want to know?"

"Ten years ago, there was a party at the Plaza. It was Jack Roch's birthday party. After the party, he went back to his penthouse with a few of his more select guests. Among them were America's sweethearts, Jane Morley and Danny Santos, and their agent, Henry Silva. It was our understanding at the time that these three people were together the whole evening, but it now seems that was not the case, and Mr. Roch had arranged two companions to spend the night with Danny Santos. I have been told that you might know something about that, even though it was ten years ago. Is that right?"

She took a moment, but I didn't get the impression she was thinking about her answer, rather it was the phrasing she was turning over. In the end, she looked down at her knee, ran her finger over her leggings, and said, "Yes."

I waited, but apparently that was all she was saying.

"I need you to tell me everything you know. Were you there in person?"

She nodded several times slowly. "Yes."

I waited a moment, then prompted her. "So...?"

She took a deep breath. "So I was eighteen. My roommates and I received a call from our agent."

"Your agent?"

She closed her eyes a moment and gave an unhappy smile. "You might call her a madam. She looked after us, got us off the streets, and arranged high-class clients for us. We made a great deal of money. In any other profession, she would be called an agent."

"I understand."

"Our agent told us she had booked us for a gig at an address in Manhattan. I can't tell you the address, but I am pretty sure, under the circumstances, any surmise you make will be accurate."

"Okay, so what were the terms of the gig?"

"There were three of us, and the client wanted us to entertain two friends of his. One of them she said had peculiar tastes but was not violent or aggressive. That friend turned out to be Danny Santos. My friend and I were pretty happy and more than willing to cater to what we assumed were his tastes."

I frowned. "What do you mean what you assumed were his tastes?"

"I am not going to go into details, but what we did not expect was our champagne to be drugged. We put on a show for him—"

"Where? In front of everyone at the party?"

"No, he took us to a private room. We had a bottle of champagne, but after about ten minutes, we both started getting very sleepy. Then I don't remember anything else except that I woke up and we were being served breakfast in bed by a maid."

I sagged back in my chair. "He drugged you."

"Yes."

"Did you ever hear from him again?"

"No."

"What about your other roommate? Can you tell me what happened to her?"

She hesitated. "She was with Danny Santos' agent. Apparently, his tastes were pretty mainstream. They hit the sack, snorted some coke, drank champagne, and he fell asleep beside her while she watched a movie on TV."

I nodded. "One man's mainstream." She gave a small shrug. I went on, "Katherine, what I am about to tell you is in the public domain. I am not telling you anything you couldn't have read in a newspaper or seen on TV or Facebook."

I paused. She didn't say anything, so I went on.

"That same night, Jane Morley's personal assistant was murdered in a hotel room in the Bronx. She was beaten so badly she had several broken limbs, and then she was stabbed several times with a knife. There was a total lack of evidence, and the case went cold."

"I remember."

"Henry Silva and Jane Morley provided Danny with an alibi, and Danny and Jane provided Henry Silva with an alibi because they claimed they went together and stayed together all night. You understand that what you are telling me means that their alibis are worthless."

"I understand that Danny Santos' alibi is. Henry Silva was with my roommate. But I have made it clear you cannot use this information in court, and I will not testify. If you subpoena me, I'll say I was with him all night."

I sighed. "Okay, thinking back to that night, before you retired with Danny, can you remember what happened with Jane? Who she was with?"

She thought about it a moment, then nodded. "Yeah, I noticed because all three of us were pretty excited we were at a party with America's sweethearts. That kind of thing impresses you when you're young. Danny was draped all over me and one of my friends, and Jane was all over some young guy. I don't know who he was. He wasn't famous, but they obviously knew each other."

"You didn't catch a name?"

"No. It was a long time ago."

I was about to stand when something struck me. "If he had been a male escort, would you have known?"

She gave her head a little twitch. "Probably. High-class companions are a pretty small community in Manhattan. But in any case, he didn't come across that way. They knew each other already, judging by the way they greeted each other. I kind of assumed he was an up-and-coming actor."

We talked a little longer, going over details, and I left, not much wiser than when I had arrived.

ELEVEN

I stepped into the fresh midday sun and walked slowly with my hands thrust deep in my pockets. I went round the corner and into West 83rd, where I stood a while leaning on the roof of the old car, drumming my fingers and trying to imagine Danny Santos drugging his two high-class companions and then driving off to the Bronx to kill Kate Hagan. Did that entail a knowledge of drugs? Did he have a knowledge of drugs? Before I could get into the swing of it, though, my cell rang. It was Dehan.

"I'll talk to you about cables later, over dinner. Right now, Joe and Frank want us at the Jacobi. There are things they say they don't understand."

"Which means they do understand them but they want us to reach the same conclusions as them by walking us through it."

"Right. You pick me up on the way?"

"Sure. I'm on my way now."

"Any joy from the goddesses of pleasure?"

"Not really." I pulled open the door. "But it looks like Danny doesn't have an alibi."

"Oh, man."

"Yeah. I'll tell you when I get there. You found something useful about electrical cables?"

"Maybe."

I hung up, fired up the growler, and headed east toward the FDR.

WE FOUND Joe and Frank in Frank's small, cramped office at the mortuary. He was sitting behind his small, steel desk, surrounded by stacks of files and loose sheets of paper, and Joe was on a steel and canvas folding chair. They were drinking coffee and laughing. Frank reduced to a chuckle as we walked in.

"John, we were just talking about you. Carmen, always a pleasure. Do sit if you can find somewhere."

Carmen unfolded another chair, and I leaned against the doorjamb. "Dehan said there were things you didn't understand. I told her I didn't believe you. She agreed."

He smiled at Joe. "One acquires a godly status and this is what happens, you see?"

Joe grinned, then looked up at me. "There are some inconsistencies. The cable is professional, industrial grade electrical cable of the sort you might use in a factory—"

Dehan said, "Or a film studio."

"Certainly, and you were absolutely correct: It had traces of skin and perspiration that we were able to recover and get a DNA profile from."

I said, "That's good work, Joe. Did you get a hit?"

"We got a profile but not a hit. I can tell you it's a man, but he is not on our databases."

I looked at Dehan. She met my eye. "That fits."

Frank asked, "What does?"

"Stone just found out Danny Santos' alibi for the night of Kate's murder isn't worth the two high-class hookers it was based on. His DNA would not be on any database, as far as I know."

"Well, I guess you need to find out where he was yesterday afternoon and get him to spit at you or something. Is he given to spitting or dribbling?"

He stood as he asked the question and came around the desk, headed for his autopsy room. I narrowed my eyes as he edged past.

"Not that I am aware of, Frank, but I just know you have a reason for that question."

He led the way to one of the steel autopsy tables where a body lay under a sheet. He pulled the sheet back to reveal Silva's lifeless body. The face was a patchy yellow and purple, as was the bruise around his throat. Frank pointed at the forehead and the area of left cheek and the bridge of the nose.

"He had saliva on his face. The killer either spat at him while he was killing him, or he dribbled. You know people in a murderous frenzy will sometimes expel saliva through their teeth."

"That's an image I am going to try hard to forget, Frank."

"Yes, well, it happens. The killer then evidently tried to wipe it off but didn't make a great job of it. The traces were there, as I say, on the forehead, the bridge of the nose, and his left cheek."

He pulled over a chair on wheels from one of the benches and spun it around.

"Sit."

I sat, and he stood behind me. He took a large handkerchief from his pocket, spun it so it formed a cord, and put it around my neck.

"He is in this position, pulling hard because Silva is a strong man. Silva is leaning back from the pressure on his throat—lean back!—and the killer is leaning forward, thus." He leaned over me slightly. "And with the murderous effort, he dribbles, or out of hatred and contempt, he spits."

He released the handkerchief, and I stood, rubbing my neck. Dehan was grinning at me. "How does it feel to be dribbled on, Stone?"

I shrugged. "Nothing new. I'm used to it." I turned to Joe. "So does the saliva match with the skin traces on the cable?"

It was Frank who answered. "It was the same guy."

I shrugged and frowned. "So what is it you don't understand?"

Joe crossed his arms and went up on his toes. "Well, John, in this age of Woke, we are supposed to take these things in our stride and not question them, but statistics and the guy in the street are not as in tune with Wokery as the Woke community would like us to believe."

My frown deepened. "What are you talking about?"

"You told me to have a look behind the living room door because whoever clubbed you came out of that door, you remember?"

"Sure."

"Well, we went over the area, and we found a short, blond hair, but we found other things too. There were a couple of whiskey tumblers in the kitchen sink, along with a sponge scourer that had dish soap on it. The faucet was open. The impression was the killer, or whomever it was, was about to wash the glasses when you arrived. An analysis of the saliva on the glasses gave us Silva for one and the killer on the second."

Dehan said, "The same as the skin and the saliva."

"Correct. But here is where it gets complicated. The killer's glass had lipstick on it."

I screwed up my brow and sat slowly in the wheeled chair again. I saw the turmoil in my head expressed on Dehan's face. Her mouth worked silently for a moment, then, "He was disguised as a woman?"

I shook my head. "No."

Joe shrugged. "You guys are the detectives, but Silva let him in..."

Frank snorted. "Danny Santos dressed as a woman would stand out like a sore thumb. Most men do. Much easier and less risky to wear a fake beard or a wig and sunglasses."

"But..."

"Now you see," he went on, "why I said we didn't understand."

Dehan held up both hands. "Wait! What are the logical options?"

Frank didn't know Dehan well enough to know that meant *Shut up and listen, I am about to list our options.* He gave a small shrug.

"Well, one: a man dressed as a woman for either, A, the purpose of disguise or B, a sexual proclivity such as being a transvestite or a transsexual or whatever we are supposed to call them today. Two, there was a woman accompanying the killer and she drank whiskey while he did not, or three, the killer wore lipstick for some personal reason of his own. Anything beyond those three options I think is bordering the realms of fantasy."

Dehan tried to smile and failed. "Thanks, Frank. My problem is trying to fit our extremely small pool of suspects into any of those categories. Danny Santos is not a transsexual—"

"In any case"—it was Frank interrupting her again—"a DNA test will give you the gender a person is born with, not the one they attempt to assume. So if Danny Santos had started life as a woman, which he did not, his DNA sample would show him as a woman, not a man."

"Right, neither is he insane enough, as far as we know, to come and visit his agent wearing lipstick, much less dressed as a woman. These people are all about protecting the sacred cash cow that is America's sweethearts. I can't believe he would take a risk like that."

Joe gave his head a small twitch. "If he's your guy, he sure took a risk at the party."

She stared at him for a long moment with no expression on her face. I knew she was struggling with a gut feeling that completely contradicted what logic dictated. She turned to me.

"Stone?"

I raised my shoulders a fraction. "I guess we'll have to explore Danny Santos' sexual proclivities, and also snoop around their social circle and see if they have any male friends who use lipstick. In New York arty circles, I guess that's not as unusual as you might expect."

She nodded. "Yeah." She stared for a moment at the body on the dissection table. "So did he just start using lipstick recently? Or was he using it back when he killed Kate in a totally different way?"

I sighed heavily and stood. "Come on, I need some lunch and a beer, and you need a green tea."

"There is one other thing." It was Frank. "Joe, help me to turn him over, will you?"

Between them, they turned Silva's body over on his face. Rigor had set in, and he had the unsettling appearance of a cardboard mannequin. When the body was settled on its face, Frank pointed to the bare back. There were a couple of dark purple marks, one on the right shoulder, the other a little below it.

"See these? You asked me to look for something like this. They might explain why he remained seated while he was being strangled."

"A Taser?"

"Or some similar devise capable of delivering a paralyzing electrical discharge. My guess is he wandered behind him while they were talking, paralyzed him with a couple of jolts from the weapon, then put the cable around his neck and strangled him. Silva never had a chance to respond."

Dehan was shaking her head. "No, this is not the same guy. This is a different MO completely. This guy is all about electricity. The cable, the zapper, and he has sexual proclivities. He wears lipstick, for crying out loud. The guy who killed Kate Hagan was just a guy. He was jealous or he was scared she was going to expose their relationship. Normal guy stuff. So he beat her into submission and stabbed her to death. Normal guy murder." She gestured at the body. "Whoever did this is like a Woke nerd with proclivity issues!"

Frank shrugged and spread his hands.

"If I believed in God, I would thank Him for making you the detectives and me the ME. I work out how he died. You have to work out how he was killed, and what's worse, *why* he was killed."

THE AFTERNOON WAS GROWING OLD. The sun, low in the south, cast a chill amber glow, and the trees in the Jacobi parking lot cast long, sleepy shadows. Dehan took my right arm in both of hers, and I shoved my hands in my pockets as we ambled toward the old Jag.

"It can't be a coincidence." She looked up at me, and I nodded agreement. "It would be off the chart that these two murders are completely unconnected."

"I agree. They are connected. I'd go further. I'd say Silva was murdered *because* we are investigating Kate's murder."

We came to the car, and I fished out the leys. When I'd opened the door, she said, "We can't prove that yet, but I have to say I am sure you're right."

We climbed in and slammed the doors, sealing out the cold and the noise. I put the key in the ignition and paused.

"Which means that Silva knew, or came to realize, who the real killer was."

I turned the key, and the engine roared.

She groaned and flopped back in her seat. "Which takes us right back to the night of the party and their mutual alibis. It's Danny. It's got to be Danny. It doesn't make sense any…"

She trailed off. I glanced at her as I pulled onto Morris Park Avenue and headed at a stately pace toward Emilio's Pizza.

"Maybe," I said, because she had gone quiet. "Maybe he wanted to create a red herring and make us believe a woman had killed him—a jealous lover or something. Maybe it was just an incompetent ruse."

"No."

"No? Why are you so sure?"

I pulled up outside Emilio's, and we climbed out and went inside. Emilio greeted us like family, and for five minutes, we stood and talked about the joys of pregnancy, how I had to look after Dehan, the value of the institution of the family, and how it is venerated in the Mediterranean. Then we sat by the open fire, and he went to get us a beer and a green tea and two pizzas: one pepperoni and one with pineapple, cheese, anchovies, and soy sauce.

I repeated my question.

"Why are you so sure the lipstick is not a red herring?"

"Because I know who killed Silva."

TWELVE

She sipped her tea, and I pulled off half my beer.

"I mean," she said, setting down her cup carefully in the saucer, "I know on a gut level. I know I'm right, but there are problems."

"There always are. Hit me."

"What was her name? Captain Essential at the studio." She wagged her fingers at me like she wanted me to give her something. "We told her our suspicions, that Kate had become intimate with somebody, remember? She asked for your card and said she'd think about it and get in touch."

"Bella, Bella Milano, the gaffer. Electric cable and a Taser."

"Right. Short blond hair and intense enough to spit in any guy's face."

"But wait, wait, wait." I held up both hands. "What are we saying? First off, what reason would Bella have to kill Kate? And—"

"None! On the contrary, Stone. Think about it. What if Bella was falling for Kate? What if the person Kate was becoming intimate with was Bella? It's not hard to believe, Stone. This is a woman who has had no male relationships but has devoted herself to another woman for years. Maybe she was a lesbian in denial. Maybe Bella, who takes care of everything, helped her out of the closet. Maybe she and Bella fell for each other."

I thought about it. It was more than feasible.

"Kate wants to break free and make a life with her new lover. Maybe she starts making demands and/or threats. Anyhow, Silva for some reason, perceives her as a threat to America's sweethearts and kills her. The case goes cold, but something in what we said to Bella made her connect the dots, and she came up with him." I was saying it, but I knew it was wrong. I shook my head. "No."

Dehan took the words from my mouth. "No. We didn't tell her anything that would incriminate Silva. But remember she told us Jane had come to depend on her almost as much as she did on Kate? And that you didn't become indispensable without listening to gossip? Remember?"

"Yup."

"You grilled Danny and broke their collective alibi. Danny told Jane, and Jane told Bella. Somehow she knew it wasn't Danny. Maybe he's not made of the right stuff, or maybe she knows his proclivities include making out with unconscious hookers. Point is she was convinced that if the alibi was fake, Silva was her guy, and she went and paid the debt."

I was nodding a lot. The pizzas arrived, and after Emilio had gone, I shook my head at her.

"It is compelling, and I confess my gut is telling me it is really close to the truth. But we have a big problem, Dehan. The killer is a man. Bella is a woman."

"Are you sure? How do you know?"

I stared at her. "You mean she was a guy before and changed over?"

"I don't know. But it's not beyond the bounds of possibility, is it? It would not be hard to imagine her as a guy."

"No, but"—I winced and frowned—"it's a hell of a reach. Besides, she likes women. She's butch. Why would a guy become a woman if he's going to be a butch lesbian? He might as well stay a man. That doesn't make sense."

"What can I tell you, Sensei? It happens. Guys become women who are then lesbians, women become guys who are then gay. One thing is your proclivities and another is your gender."

I gazed at my pepperoni pizza for a moment and sighed. "Dehan?"

"Yuh?" She asked it with her mouth full.

"Are you ever going to stop saying proclivities?"

"No, it's become one of my linguistic proclivities."

"Okay." I cut into my pizza and picked up a wedge in my fingers. "Here is how we are going to do this. You are going to have a nice, long chat with Jane about that night at the gala and then the party at the penthouse. Tell her what we know, but bit by bit. Feed it to her piecemeal. Allow her to tangle herself in knots of contradictions."

"I know what to do."

"I know you do. What we really want to know at this stage is if Kate was threatening the America's sweethearts product. And as a bonus whether she knows if Danny or Silva left the party. Katherine Parr says Silva never left but fell asleep in the arms of his companion while she was watching a movie on TV."

"So romantic. Why can't I have a man like that? What are you going to do?"

"I am going to dig into Bella Milano's past and find out if she was ever a guy. And that is truly something I never imagined I would ever say."

"Yup, welcome to the age of Aquarius."

We went back to the station, and she sat down to call Jane. While she dialed, I started a search of the various city databases that were open to me without a warrant. It turned out Bella Milano was not such a common name. I found her on LinkedIn and on Facebook, but I didn't find her anywhere else, not in the Land Register and not on the Voters' Register. There was apparently no official trace of her.

I knew she had a job, and I knew she must pay taxes. So reluctantly, I called the studio and asked to be put through to the personnel department. A pleasant female voice answered.

"Personnel, what can I do for you?"

I made my voice as human and agreeable as I could. "This is Detective John Stone of the New York Police Department. We are looking into the murder of Jane Morley's personal assistant ten years back. You recall that?"

"Oh, sure. How can we help?"

"We are conducting some routine checks mainly for the purpose of eliminating the irrelevant, and I was wondering if you could give me some background on one of your gaffers."

"Uh, which one?" She sounded a little uncertain.

"Bella Milano. I believe she's been with you for about twenty-five years, since she was a kid."

I heard some keys rattle. Then, "Yes, and what is it you want to know about her, Detective?"

"Her Social Security number would be a start. Anything else, like her address or anything you might think is useful."

"To be honest, Detective, I don't know how I stand as far as data protection is concerned."

I put a smile in my voice and said, "I'm not asking for anything private or personal like her bank account or her medical records. Just give me whatever is in the public domain, like her Social Security number, address. I don't know if she has a parking spot. Would you happen to have a record of her vehicle license plate?"

"We do. I hope this is not going to get me into trouble."

"Not at all. Tell you what, if you're worried, just give it to me over the phone, and there'll be no record of you sending me the info. How's that?"

"Oh-kay!" She said it like she was giving herself a last warning, then she gave me a string of data, of which the most significant were Bella's Social Security number, her car, and the registration number.

When I hung up, Dehan was still on the phone. She seemed to be laughing a lot. I glanced over as she said, "And ain't that the truth. That's stuff only a woman understands, right?"

I rolled my eyes and looked down at the information I had scrawled on my pad. Bella's car was a white Honda

Accord. I tried to remember if she had been wearing lipstick when I spoke to her. I didn't think so. Would she put lipstick on to go and visit Silva? It seemed unlikely, but then we were in a new age of gender fluidity, and show biz was show biz. Maybe they had a proclivity.

Dehan was saying, "Oh, I would *love* that. But listen, Stone is giving me that look—"

I wasn't looking at her. I was looking at the words *Honda Accord*, but I did look up when she started laughing helplessly and saying, "Yeah...that one! That one!"

She crossed her eyes at me and poked out her tongue. "So back to business or I'm going to get told off. When can you make it? Oh, that would be great. Yeah, no, he won't be there. It'll be just you and me." She giggled a bit, said, "Can't wait!" and hung up.

"Tell me that was an act."

"Kind of, but she is sweet, Stone. I like her."

"I wasn't even looking at you."

"I know. Come on, don't get serious. I was creating rapport."

"So when is she coming?"

"In about an hour."

"You forming a friendship?"

She frowned at me. "No, Stone. It's just girl talk."

"We really need to know if Kate was threatening the America's sweethearts golden goose. She may not want to go there. We also need to know if Danny or Silva left the party. If Danny didn't, it means he has some pretty weird" —I hesitated and smiled—"*proclivities*. We need to break open their alibi completely and find out what each of them did."

"I know that, Stone."

"I know what Jane can be like. You have to be ruthless and not let her get to you."

"Stone—"

I held up my hands. "Okay."

"Trust me, will you?"

"Of course."

She jerked her head at my pad. "Whatcha got?"

"Bella's Social Security number and her car. She has practically no presence on any of the state databases, doesn't vote, doesn't own property, but she owns a white Honda Accord."

"That's the car you saw in the drive when you found Silva's body."

"Correct." I took a deep breath and puffed out my cheeks. Something felt wrong. I could hear alarm bells, and I couldn't tell why. "I'm going to do some digging on Bella and see how far this goes."

"Sure. You want some coffee?"

"Yeah, thanks."

"Stone?"

I looked up. "Yeah?"

"Relax. We're good. Everything's okay."

I gave a laugh that was not heartfelt. "I know. We're cool."

She nodded and went to get coffee.

After two hours and two cups of cold coffee-like liquid, I became aware that Dehan was not yet back from talking to Jane, and what I had discovered about Bella Milano amounted to a couple of scrawled lines in a notebook: She worked for a major TV company as a gaffer, she had been with that company for twenty-five years, from gofer to gaffer. She owned a house at the end of Turneur Avenue in the Bronx under the name Wilma Milano, and she was born in Bakersfield, California, on 8th Street and P Street, right between the Church of the Living God and the Pay Less Supermarket. She'd enrolled at Vista High School at age fourteen and then vanished.

A telephone conversation with the head of the school revealed that they had no record of either Wilma or Bella Milano. It also revealed that she was extremely busy and if I wanted information, I should contact the Bakersfield PD and get them to request a warrant from a Bakersfield judge.

While I was fetching myself a third cup of black liquid, I saw Jane trotting down the stairs. She was talking into a cell phone giving somebody instructions on where to pick her up. She saw me, snapped something into the phone, and hung up. She stopped in front of me, staring up into my face, then she stabbed a finger gently on my chest.

"She's too good for you."

She brushed past me and made for the door.

"Jane." She turned and looked at me. I shook my head. "No, she's not. We are both perfect for each other."

I stepped toward her and stood looking down into her face. "I can't work it out yet, but I will."

"What will you work out, John?"

"Who you're shielding." I waited, but she didn't say anything. She didn't tell me I was being absurd or ridiculous, or laugh in my face. She just stared at me. "Why you brought those letters in. Why you started up the investigation again if you wanted to shield somebody."

She let her eyes roam over me and my face.

"I brought the letters in because they were new evidence, John, and I want Kate's killer caught."

"Whoever he is?"

"Yes."

"Did Dehan ask you about Danny's proclivities?"

Her eyelids fluttered, and she backed away a step. "Leave me alone, John. I'll only deal with Carmen from now on. Don't talk to me."

She turned and hurried out of the station into the cold, late afternoon. I stood a while at the door and saw a Bentley roll up. She didn't climb in the back. She got in the front passenger seat. The door closed silently, and the car pulled away.

After a while, I felt a hand rest gently on my shoulder. I turned and saw Dehan smiling at me. It wasn't a happy smile. It was a worried smile.

"What's on your mind, Sensei?"

I looked back at the street where the Bentley had been a couple of minutes earlier.

"I am not feeling very wise at the moment, Little Grasshopper. We are missing something. Something important. And the longer we miss it, the more…"

I trailed off.

"The more what?"

I turned and looked into her eyes. "The more dangerous it becomes."

THIRTEEN

We sat facing the chief across his desk. I noticed the gray in his temples had turned white, and the curls on his head that had once been black were now getting gray flecks. Something a Buddhist said to me once flitted through my mind: "We are all masticated by the jaws of impermanence." His hair was certainly being masticated.

"Just tell me," he was saying to Dehan with a facetious smile on his face, "that you don't plan to charge Barack Obama with Kate Hagan's murder."[1]

Dehan forced a smile and shook her head. "No, we plan to charge him with the assassination of John F. Kennedy."

"Very good." He chortled. "Excellent. So what can I do for you?"

"I need to go to Bakersfield."

His smile became oddly rigid. "Bakersfield, California?"

"That one."

---

1. See *A Love to Kill For*

"It is somewhat outside your jurisdiction, John."

"It's complicated, sir. We have reason to suspect somebody who is close to Jane Morley. The problem is she is a woman, but the forensic evidence which points to her in every other way also says she's a man."

"Oh, dear God."

"I have tried to get what information I can about her from the various city databases, but there is very little. I know she was born in Bakersfield, and she disappeared from her high school there when she was fifteen, about twenty-five years ago. However, when I contacted her high school, they claim to have no record of her."

He grunted. "This case..." He trailed off, then gave a bitter laugh. "I'd almost prefer you charged Barack Obama. This case is delicate on so many levels."

"That is part of the reason why I want to go there myself, sir. If I requested help from Bakersfield PD, I would have to go into so much detail just to get them to understand the questions I need to ask and *whom* I need to ask. The potential for the whole thing to explode in our face is huge."

"Whom, yes..." He said it absently, gazing at his window. Then he shifted his eyes back to me. "Whom?" he said. "Whom are you going to ask?"

"I know where she was born."

"Or he."

"Or he. I want to see, very discreetly, if his or her parents are still living there. I also want to go to his school and speak to the director in person and see why they have no record of that pupil. Whatever I learn from those two sources will determine where I go from there."

He turned to Dehan. "Will you accompany him, Carmen?"

"No, he won't let me."

I said, "Sir, the other angle in this case involves Danny Santos. Initially, Danny and Henry Silva, his agent, gave each other mutual alibis along with Jane Morley. The night Kate was killed, they all went to a gala together, and then they went to a party at Jack Roch's apartment. The three of them alleged that they were in each other's company all night."

He frowned. "But...?"

"But when I started probing, I found a reliable witness who told us that they were not in each other's company at all. More to the point, nobody can account for Danny Santos' movements that night because he drugged the two hookers he was with, and they were unconscious all night."

"Dear God. Who is this witness?"

"One of the hookers, but she was provided to us by the Bureau on the condition we did not use her. If we do, she will deny everything, and we'll have an army of judges, congressmen, and billionaires clamoring for our blood."

He narrowed his eyes at me, and his lips moved silently until he expostulated, "Other detectives just catch ordinary murderers. With you there is always..." He trailed off.

"Maybe that's why the case went cold. I just follow the evidence, sir."

"Yes, of course." He sighed. "Forgive me, John. I shall have to contact Bakersfield Police Department out of common courtesy. But do please be very discreet. The last thing we need is a Woke lobby clamoring for our blood."

"I'll be discreet, sir. But while I am gone, Dehan is going

to be—" I paused and hesitated. "She's going to be looking into Danny Santos' alibi."

He took a deep breath and heaved an unhappy sigh. "Very well. Make the booking. And you, Carmen." He turned to look at her. "Please be careful."

―――

Twenty-four hours later, I was sitting in my rental in the parking lot of the Pay Less Supermarket, watching the house where Bella Milano had been born. It was pretty much everything I had expected. It was a low, one-story building with a low, gabled roof. It was surrounded by an unkempt, yellowing lawn, and that in turn was surrounded by a chicken wire fence attached to a steel tubing frame. The gate was the same. No white pickets here.

I climbed out of the car and crossed the road at a trot. I unlatched the gate. It gave a metallic creak, and before I had crossed the lawn to the porch, I saw the drapes move in the window.

I rang the bell. After a long pause, the door opened an inch, held by a chain.

"Who is it?"

It was a voice that had been frightened too often to be nice.

"Good afternoon. Mrs. Milano?"

"Who wants to know?"

I showed her my badge. "My name is Detective John Stone. I'm from the New York Police Department."

The shadowy figure peering through the crack in the door scowled. "*New York?*"

"I'm here at the invitation of the Bakersfield Police Department, ma'am. I was wondering if I could ask you a few questions."

"What about? I ain't got nothin' to tell the New York cops."

I smiled. "I understand that, ma'am, but as I say, I am here at the invitation of the Bakersfield PD, and if you could spare me five minutes now, it would save us all a lot of hassle later."

"Hassle? What hassle?"

"Well, you know, court orders, warrants, material witness… all that stuff that nobody really wants."

I didn't tell her the court orders, warrants, and material witness status did not necessarily involve her, but she seemed to assume they did because a moment later she unlatched the door to scowl at me.

"Harassment and threats. Police state. That's what this country is comin' to. Like Soviet fuckin' Russia."

"I only need five minutes of your time, ma'am, and I'll be on my way."

"You can't come in. If I scream, I want the neighbors to hear me. What do you want to know?"

"Do you have a daughter named Bella Milano?"

"No. What else?"

"What about Wilma?"

"No. You're wasting your time and mine. I ain't got no kids."

"But you have lived at this address for—"

"I was born at this address, and I'll die at this address! And there ain't nothin' you can do about it! It's *my* house!"

"Yes, ma'am. That's absolutely right. But—"

"I don't need you"—she stabbed a long, crooked finger at me—"to tell me I have the right to be in my own home!"

"Absolutely not, Mrs. Milano. I just want to know—"

"Pryin' into people's private lives!"

"Did you—"

"Fuck off and mind your own business before I call the *real* cops!"

She slammed the door, and a moment later, I saw her peering at me from behind her drapes. I decided a tactical retreat was in order and crossed the road back to my car. There I sat drumming my fingers on the steering wheel and wishing I could talk to Dehan. Dehan, I decided, would have known how to turn on the charm and get around her. My options now were to ask a favor of the local PD, which they were unlikely to grant given the flimsy nature of my evidence, or withdraw and take a completely different tack.

I fired up the car, which was a Honda Accord, and drove slowly down P Street toward Vista High School.

It was fenced in with the same chicken wire and steel tubing as Mrs. Milano's house, giving it more the look and feel of a prison than a school. I smiled to myself as I parked. In my head, I could hear Dehan making some comment about a society where the kids go to prison for their education. The schools she had looked at in Maine hadn't looked like prisons.

I pulled my cell and called the school.

"Good afternoon, Vista High School, how may I help you?"

"Good afternoon. This is Detective John Stone from the New York Police Department. I have flown in from New York at the invitation of the Bakersfield Police Department, and I would very much like to speak to the principal of your school. I am sitting outside your gate right now. It is a matter of some urgency."

She was silent for a moment, then said, "Please hold."

After some thirty seconds, another voice came on the line. It was a woman's voice that had grown severe on its own authority.

"Detective Stone, this is Principal Marshall. Could you not have called and made an appointment? I am extremely busy."

"So am I, Principal Marshall. And I have just flown two and a half thousand miles to be here. I don't know how Bakersfield PD operates, but in New York, we only do that if it is a matter of urgency. We are conducting a murder inquiry in which two people have been killed already. It would be nice if you could find ten minutes to help us to avoid a third killing, particularly as the victim might be one of your alumni."

There was a sigh. "There is no need for sarcasm, Detective. Naturally we will help if we can. You say you are outside."

"I am outside your main gate. I will take up as little of your time as I am able. I am anxious to get back to New York."

"Please drive through to reception."

A few seconds later, the gate buzzed open, and I drove through.

There was a small office in the lobby. There was a woman in the doorway whose heavy glasses made her look angry, like the whole damn world was misbehaving. She approached me on little stamping feet and said, "I take it you are Detective Stone."

I couldn't think of a wiseass answer, so I said, "Yes."

She pointed over to my left. "Please take that elevator to the top floor. As you step out, turn left. The principal's office is at the end. Please be as brief as possible. The principal is a *very* busy woman."

I regarded her with diminishing patience. As she turned to leave, I said, "You know who was a really busy woman?"

She looked at me in alarm. Maybe she wasn't used to being asked questions she didn't know the answer to.

"What?"

"Kate Hagan. Kate Hagan was a very busy woman. Never stopped. Eighteen hours a day. Never missed a day, and her work was flawless, all the time."

Her mouth worked resentfully. "I have no idea what you're—"

"She's not busy anymore." I cut her dead. "Do you know why she isn't busy anymore?" She made a sort of "B-b-b" noise, which I ignored. "She isn't busy because she's dead. Somebody beat her until her bones broke, and then, when she was helpless and couldn't move, they stabbed her to death. Maybe you think the cops shouldn't waste their time or anybody else's solving that kind of crime. But then again, maybe some day your daughter or your granddaughter might get raped or beaten or murdered, and some stuck-up, self-important cow will refuse to assist the cops in their investigation, and you'll remember this day and regret your arrogant stupidity."

Her eyes went huge behind her large glasses, and her

mouth sagged open. I gave her a little nod. "Thanks for your help."

I rode the elevator to the third floor, stepped out, and turned left. There was a long, depressing corridor, and at the end, there was a door painted blue. I approached it wondering to myself why government institutions tried so hard to be depressing. I knocked, and the door was yanked open almost immediately by a woman in a blue cardigan with a double string of pearls hung around her neck. She had an expression on her face that said she was waiting for the next problem in life so she could give it a hard time.

"Detective Stone?"

"Yes." I showed her my badge. "Good afternoon."

She arched an eyebrow at me. "Come in. I can spare you fifteen minutes."

I tried to stifle the sigh but didn't do a very good job.

"Principal Marshall, I don't know what kind of person you are, whether you have any moral fiber at all, whether you give a damn about a woman being beaten to a pulp and then stabbed to death. Perhaps you're the kind of person who believes that other people's suffering is other people's problem. I don't know, and frankly I don't care. Nearly thirty years on the force has shown me that scum comes in all kinds of shapes and sizes and occupies all kinds of offices. But I have to tell you that you will spare me as long as I need. If not today, tomorrow at the local station or in New York with cuffs on your wrists as a material witness."

She stood behind her desk with her hands on her chair staring at her blotter. I knew she was fighting her anger, and I knew I had crossed a line, but the truth was right then I didn't give a damn. I closed the door and went and stood across from her, mirroring her, with my hands on the back of the chair where I would sit.

"Kate Hagan, Jane Morley's personal assistant, was lured into a hotel room, beaten to a pulp until most of her bones were broken, and as she lay there desperately in need of help, somebody stabbed her several times until she was dead."

She drew breath, but I wasn't done yet.

"A couple of days ago, Jane Morley and Danny Santos' agent, you know, America's sweethearts, their agent, he was found strangled to death in his den with a strip of electrical cable round his throat. He had been electrocuted with a Taser first so he'd be paralyzed while he was being strangled. Now it seems to me that the principal of a public school should probably be the kind of person who gives a damn about that sort of thing. But who am I to judge? All I want you to realize is that if I think you have information I need, in a case like this, you are going to give me that information if it takes ten minutes, sixteen minutes, sixteen hours, or if I have to bring a dozen cars here with their sirens blaring and their lights flashing to take you down to the station. Do we understand each other?"

She pulled out her chair and sat, watching me with hostile eyes. I sat opposite her.

"Detective Stone, you spoke to my secretary the other day, and she has already told you—"

"You want to let me ask you my questions? That way we'll finish sooner."

She took a deep breath. "What do you want to know?"

I smiled unpleasantly. "If we had started there, we'd probably be done by now."

FOURTEEN

"We have no record, Detective Stone, of anyone by the name of Bella or Wilma Milano at this school at the end of the '90s or at the beginning of the millennium. And I would be grateful if you stopped your personal attacks on me."

"Yeah, Kate Hagan would probably empathize with you. And if you'll stop telling me what I already know, perhaps I can tell you why I have traveled two and a half thousand miles across a continent to speak to you." I paused. She didn't answer. I went on. "It is possible that the person in question had a sex change—"

"I think you'll find they are referred to as gender reassignments these days, Detective."

"By whom, Principal Marshall? Right-thinking people? Are we done measuring genders, Principal Marshall?"

She closed her eyes and sighed. She was probably counting to ten. I went on.

"So back then, this person might have been called Bill or William. For all I know, he might have been called Geronimo or Leovigild, but if he attended this school at the turn of the millennium and his home address was at the corner of P Street and 8th Street, there is a damned good chance it's the same person."

She hesitated. "I'm not sure..."

I leaned forward, trying hard to contain an anger that was welling up inside me, though I wasn't sure exactly where it was coming from.

"This person may be at risk. Two people have died already. If you refuse to help me and because of that delay another person dies, I will hold you personally responsible. Why don't you give the right thinking a rest, Principal Marshall, and try thinking like a human being for a change. Help me to avoid another murder!"

Her face flushed, and she reached for the telephone.

"Shanice, will you please check student records for '98, '99, and the first two years of the millennium? We are looking for a boy with the surname Milano. He might be William or Bill, but not necessarily. His address will be P Street and 8th. The detective will come and collect whatever you have in a moment." She hung up. "Is there anything else I can do for you, Detective?"

I stood. "It's not for me. It's for another human being who might be needlessly killed. But don't worry about it. It's not your problem. You've done as much as the law requires of you."

I made my way to the door with an irrational anger welling in my gut. I stopped with my hand on the handle and turned back to her.

"If you have trouble sleeping, Marshall, try not looking at yourself in the mirror before you go to bed."

I left before she could answer and went down in the elevator wondering why I had allowed her to get to me like that.

I went into the office and found the woman with heavy glasses sitting at one computer and a young black girl sitting at another. She looked up as I came in and smiled.

"You Detective Stone?"

"I am. Are you Shanice?"

She got up and went to a printer, where she took a piece of paper and brought it over to me.

"You're from New York?"

I nodded. "The Bronx."

"Man I miss that place. I grew up there. Nowhere like it." She put the sheet of paper in front of me. "William Boyd Milano, joined the school in '98 aged fifteen. He stayed one year, failed all his exams, and never came back. Address 911 8th Street."

In the top left corner, there was a small photograph of Bella Milano as she must have looked at fifteen. I nodded.

"Thanks, that's really helpful."

She gave me a lopsided smile, leaning on the counter. "What precinct you at?"

"Fteley Avenue, 43rd. You know it?"

"Bailed my dad and my brother out a couple of times. Guess it's as well I moved. You might have ended up arresting me sometime."

I shook my head. "It's about the choices you make, not where you make them. You're smart enough to make good choices. You would have made them back home too."

"Yeah, guess you're right at that. Hang loose, Detective."

"You too, Shanice."

I turned right out of the gate onto P Street and made my way back toward Mrs. Milano's house. I stopped outside, climbed out of the car, and crossed the lawn to her window. I could see her staring out at me, and I shoved the piece of paper Shanice had given me up against the glass. I mouthed at her, "*Open the door. We need to talk!*"

She stared at it with wide eyes in the shadows of her living room, then hurried away. After a moment, I heard the door open, and she peered out at me.

"Who are you?"

I stepped onto the porch. "Mrs. Milano, I am a policeman from New York, and I am trying to help your son."

"Help him? Why? I haven't seen him since..." Her eyes glazed.

"How long? Twenty years?"

"More. He went away."

"Bill—"

"William. I don't like Bill."

"He was at the high school for the first year."

Her eyes met mine for a moment. "He was crazy."

She turned and went inside, but she left the door open. I figured that was as close as I was going to get to an invitation. So I followed and closed the door behind me.

The door gave directly onto the living room. She moved to a chair beside an electrical heater and sat. Her hands were clasped in her lap, and her eyes frowned at me.

"Have you found him?"

I sat opposite her and nodded. "Yes. He's in New York."

"He always wanted to go to New York. He used to say you can be yourself in New York. I asked him, 'Who the hell are you in Bakersfield'? He said, 'Whoever the hell you want me to be.' Well, that ain't no way to talk to your mother, is it?"

"No."

"These days, they talk however the hell they like, kids."

"Who did he want to be, Mrs. Milano?"

"He was crazy."

"Did he tell you he was leaving?"

"He just went to school and never come back. Fuckin' bastard. Just like his dad. Crazy."

"Was he seeing a doctor? Did he ever mention a doctor to you?"

"What kind of doctor?"

"Any kind of doctor. Did he ever mention seeing a doctor or going to a clinic?"

"He never saw no doctor. He just went to school one day and never come back."

I spent another fifteen minutes with her, but that was about all she was able to give me.

In my car, I called Dehan.

"Yeah? What's up? Any news?"

"Yeah, Bella was Bill. He dropped out of high school at fifteen and disappeared. Probably went to New York. What I am not clear about is where and when he had the operation. Can you check and see if there is a federal association of gender reassignment surgeons or something similar? I want to know where and when he took that step."

"Sure, I can do that, but do you think it matters? What we really need is a sample of his DNA."

I took a deep breath and held it. When I finally released it, I said, "Yeah, I know. It will be his DNA. I'm just …*uncomfortable*. You get anywhere with Jane and Danny?"

"Not really. She's sharp as a needle."

"Yeah? What makes you say that?"

"When you were a kid, did you ever try to catch a fish with your hands? She's like that."

"Yeah, that sounds like Jane. Either way, Dehan, even if we prove Bella killed Silva, that doesn't let Silva or Danny off the hook as far as Kate is concerned."

"I know, I remember."

"Is she getting to you?"

"No, Stone! Stop asking that. I'm working on them. When are you back?"

"I'll get the next flight back."

"You okay?"

I shook my head slowly like she could see me, and after a moment I said, "Nope."

"What's on your mind?"

"I don't know. You be careful with Danny and Bella, will you? You going to see Jane before I get back?"

"This evening. She asked me to go over to her place. She wants to talk about you."

"Does she know we're married?"

"Yeah. I thought I'd better tell her. She was getting pretty intense, and I felt like I had to draw a line."

I grunted. "Be careful, Dehan. There is something about this whole setup that troubles me."

She was quiet for a moment. "Bella and Danny, right?"

"Yeah, I think so." Then I added, "Maybe don't go, Dehan. Maybe call her and tell her you don't feel great. Just go home and lock the place down. I'll be back in a few hours."

"You're really spooked, huh, Stone?"

I nodded. "Yeah, and I can't tell you why. I got an alarm bell going like crazy, but I can't tell you why. Will you go home and lock up?"

"Yeah, sure. I'll call and cancel. You want me to meet you at the airport?"

"No. I'm fine. Just go home. It must be late there by now."

"Coming up on eight p.m."

"Go home."

"Okay."

"I'm headed for the airport."

We said goodbye, and I pulled away, trying hard to stay within the speed limit.

FIFTEEN

When I came out of arrivals at JFK, Jane was waiting for me. For some reason, that gave me an adrenaline twist in my gut. She approached me among the crowd.

"Hello, John."

"What are you doing here?"

"Carmen told me you'd be arriving on this flight."

"What the hell did she do that for?"

She gave a small, humorless laugh. "Ever the charmer. I told her I needed to talk to you. She said you'd be arriving from California at this time. Is that a crime?"

"No, of course not." I started moving toward the exit for the parking lot. "What do you want?"

She took hold of my elbow and stopped me, forcing me to face her.

"Why are you so hostile to me, John? What have I done to you? We both agreed it was best to split up."

I looked down at her beautiful face and felt anger—an anger I couldn't explain or even understand. I spoke quietly.

"I don't like the way you treat people, Jane. You measure the value of people according to how useful they are to you. Yes"—I gave a couple of nods—"we split up by mutual agreement, but we were both on our way anyhow. You because you had found Henry Silva, who was way more useful to you than a Bronx detective. Me because I had come to see who you really were. I had seen that the only reason you hooked up with me in the first place was that there was nothing better available at the time, and you needed somebody to adulate you. And I had also seen that you had absolutely nothing to give. The most you could offer was for both of us to fall on our knees and adore you together."

Her voice was barely a whisper. "John, that's not true. How can you say that?"

"Not true? One of your closest friends, a woman who devoted her life to helping you become one of the greatest stars in America, is brutally beaten and stabbed to death, and you conceal evidence from the cops? You claim you were wracked for months and barely recovered, and all the while you and Silva and Danny are colluding in a false alibi? And now, Silva, the man who had been your lover, the man who elevated you to even greater heights, has been murdered, and you are palling up with Dehan like nothing has happened. For what reason, Jane? How do you think Dehan can help you? What benefit do you think you'll get?"

"John, that's—you're twisting things."

There were tears in her eyes. I told myself she was a good actress.

"I don't like the way you treat people, Jane. I don't like the fact that you don't even realize they are people. So I am asking you, what do you want?"

Before she could answer, I jerked my head toward the plate glass doors. "I have my car out there. Ride with me. You can have one of your servants come and collect yours."

She followed me in silence through the chilly early sun until we reached the Jag. I slung my bag in the trunk and climbed in behind the wheel. She hesitated a moment before getting in beside me. Maybe she thought I'd open the door for her.

I pulled out of the lot and headed for I-678. As I drove, I asked her again, "What do you want, Jane? Why did you come here to meet me?"

She was quiet, looking out the side window at the massive concrete wall covered in tumbling green and red ivy. After a while, she said, "I told you. I wanted to know why you were so hostile. I had no idea you hated me so much."

"Let me know when you're done with the drama and you can tell me why you are really here."

She shook her head at me. "You are such a bastard. You always were." I didn't react, and finally she asked me, "Why did you go to California?"

"Did you ask Dehan that question?"

"Yes."

"What did she tell you?"

"That it was part of an investigation in process and she couldn't tell me."

"But you thought if you tickled my fancy I might break the rules for you? You are badly mistaken, Jane. Instead of trying to get inside information on a murder investigation, you need to be finding ways to persuade me not to book you for providing two men with false alibis. You have no idea, you cannot begin to understand how mad I am at you for that. Do you understand—do you give a *damn*—that Henry Silva is dead because of you?"

Her mouth dropped, and her eyes went wide. "John! That's not true!"

"Your lie paralyzed the investigation, Jane! It was paralyzed for ten years until I managed to find out that you and Danny and Silva separated as soon as you arrived at the gala and did not see each other again until dawn. You had no idea where Silva or Danny were all night!"

"But surely you can't suspect…"

"Why? Why not? Somebody does."

"What do you mean?"

I half shouted at her, "Why the hell do you think Silva was murdered?"

"I don't…" She trailed off, shaking her head.

"You don't *give* a damn! Is that what you were going to say? You don't stop to think about things you don't care about, right? And you don't care about Silva just like you didn't care about Kate! All you damn-well care about is you! So that's all you damn-well think about!"

"John, will you *please* stop this!"

"*Why did you lie about Danny Santos and Henry Silva? Why did the three of you collude to lie to the cops?*"

We merged onto the expressway headed for the Bronx. After a moment, she said, "Have you any idea, have you any *conception* what it would have done to America's sweethearts if it had come out that Danny and I were in an open relationship? Not only that, but if it had emerged, during a murder investigation, that I had been Henry's lover, and that the three of us were *fucking different people that night!*" She took a deep, shaky breath.

"Have you any idea what it would do to us if it got out that Danny had a thing for screwing unconscious hookers?"

I arched an eyebrow at her. "He had what?"

She sighed heavily and looked away again. The concrete wall at the side of the road had been replaced by occasional wooded areas and snatches of suburbia.

"Danny, like most actors, is a narcissist. He is fundamentally a weak, ineffectual man who is in love with his pathetic little self. Consequently he cannot perform with a woman who demands anything of him. So he likes his women unconscious. Not only that; they must be hookers who make no emotional demands on him. Love is not part of the deal."

I was quiet for a moment, like I was thinking. I wasn't. My mind was blank. Finally I said, "So the night that Kate was killed…"

"He was screwing two unconscious whores."

"How do you know that?"

"Because Jack Roch told us he had ordered the girls from his regular supplier."

I stared at her. "*Ordered* them from his regular *supplier?* Are you kidding me? What, like steak?"

"Only more tender. That's how green the grass is on this side, John."

"Did you see him with them?"

"I was a little busy myself."

"With Simon. Did you buy him by the pound too?"

She smiled. "Is that jealousy I am hearing, John?"

"No, Jane, just disgust. So you can't provide either your husband or Silva with an alibi for that night."

She looked up at the ceiling of the car like she was counting to ten.

"You cannot seriously believe that Danny or Henry was capable of killing Kate."

"Jane, let me make this very clear for you. As far as I am concerned, people like you, people in your circle, are capable of killing their own mothers in order to protect their position at the top of the manure heap."

She drew breath. I snapped at her, "Shut up and listen! Do I believe that Danny might have been having an affair with Kate? It's possible. Do I believe Silva might have been having an affair with her? It's also possible. Do I believe that she might have used that, or the information she had about the truth behind America's sweethearts to blackmail the three of you? It is certainly possible.

"Kate had insisted on a king bed at the hotel where she was found. So she was planning to sleep with someone that night. Could it have been Henry Silva or your husband? Sure. Might they have killed her? Absolutely. So in answer to your question, yes. Danny Santos is currently at the top of our suspect list."

"Dear God..." I waited. After a moment, she said, "List... Who else is on that list?"

I didn't answer. After a while, she turned to face me. "John, why did you go to California?"

"Forget it."

"John, it's not idle curiosity. It might really be important. I need to know. Will you just once in your life not be obstinate and listen to me? If you went for the reason I think you did, I might…" She closed her eyes. "I don't want to say anything. It's probably absolute garbage, but if you went for the reason I think you went…" She trailed off again.

I glanced at her. "Why do you think I went?"

"Was it to check into somebody's past?"

"You know about it?"

"It's what I dreaded."

"Give me the name."

She covered her face with her hands. "I don't want to believe it. Poor Kate."

I spoke with savage anger snarling in my voice. "*Tell me the name!*"

She looked at me with fear in her eyes. I could see the shine of tears on her cheeks.

"Bella?"

I swore softly under my breath. She said, "Do you suspect Bella?"

"What do you know about her?"

"Always answer a question with a question, huh?"

"I'm asking the questions, Jane. Answer me. What do you know about her?"

She sighed again. Her bottom lip curled in, and she reached in her purse for a handkerchief. She dabbed her eyes and blew her nose.

"You must have noticed she is gay. Well, it goes deeper than that. She showed up—gosh, it must be twenty years ago, more—fifteen or sixteen years old, pretty, young, but obviously butch and a total lost soul."

She gave a sudden laugh.

"She was such a character! She got right past security and into the studio claiming to be my niece. She had to see me; it was of vital importance! In the end, Ned, that was the head of security at the time, he brought her to me in the dressing room. I told him to leave us, and she told me her story."

We were crossing the Union Turnpike, coming down toward the vast stretch of the Jamaica Train Yard on our left, with Willow Lake in the distance.

"What was her story?"

"She never knew her father. From what she told me, her mother was a bit crazy. It was only as she talked that I began to realize she was a boy."

"She was a boy?"

"She had boobs." She cupped her hands in front of her breasts, like I might not know what boobs were. "And as we talked, she told me she was seeing a doctor who was giving her hormones. She told me she was artistic and creative, but her home and her school stifled her and were driving her crazy. She was going to be sixteen in a month. Would I give her a job."

"So you gave her a job."

"Of course. I couldn't turn her out knowing her story and how vulnerable she was."

Meadow Lake slid past in the morning sun. Jane took a deep breath and continued.

"She worked hard. She was diligent, punctual, committed, and totally devoted. She worked her way up, year after year and became frankly indispensable to the whole crew. We all adore her."

"But?"

"But, how can I explain this, John. It's very hard, especially with you being so hostile. For a time—I don't know how long because I really didn't pay much attention, especially while she was young. I mean sixteen, seventeen, a teenager. You know they get terrible crushes at that sort of age, but it passes."

"She had a big crush on you."

"Yes, at first. But as she got older, in her twenties, she and Kate became close. I mean as friends. Obviously they saw a lot of each other at the studio, and nobody questioned it. I mean, I certainly didn't read anything into it. I think, in the beginning, there *was* nothing in it. Mainly, I think, because Kate was so devoted to her job and to me."

"That changed?"

"I think when Kate turned forty. Bella was thirty, more or less. And I suppose, in retrospect, it should have been obvious to me that Kate was a repressed lesbian. She never showed the slightest interest in men, and she devoted her life to me. I suppose sometimes you just don't see what's right in front of your nose, do you?"

I didn't say anything, but I agreed wholeheartedly.

"You kept asking who she had started seeing, whether anyone had come into her life, had her routine changed? Well, no. Everything went on as normal, but the intimacy between Kate and Bella had deepened. You know in show business, we are all very excessive in how we express our emotions. We are always hugging and kissing. I suppose nobody noticed that Bella and Kate had become close. Bella is very pushy, and Kate was ready to yield."

"How do you know all this?"

"Don't be cross."

"Cut the crap, Jane, or I swear I'll book you!"

"God! You're insufferable! I *observed* it! I knew them both intimately! I saw them fall in love with each other!"

"And why the *hell* didn't you tell me about this?"

"Because there is no way in the world that Bella is capable of murder! Just as I know for a fact that Danny and Henry are incapable of murder!"

"In Silva's case, was. Because he is dead, murdered by one of those people you say are incapable of murder."

"I don't believe it."

"Yeah, well, denial was always something you were good at. But if it wasn't Danny, it wasn't Silva, and it wasn't Bella, what the hell happened? She booked an extra big bed for her imaginary bunny, who came to life and beat her to death?"

"*John!*" She looked genuinely horrified.

We drove in silence then for a while. At Flushing Meadows, I took I-495 and headed west toward Manhattan. She noted the change in direction and smiled. She made it a vulnerable smile.

"I thought maybe you were taking me home to have lunch with you and Carmen."

"I'm going to the studio. You want me to drop you somewhere?"

"The studio is fine." She paused, then, "So why did you go to California, John?"

"To confirm a suspicion that Bella had been born a boy. Something you could have clarified for us ten years ago."

"I'm sorry."

The voice in my head told me too little too late. To her I said, "You had better wise up, Jane. This is not a game, and it's not a movie. You really need to think about the fact that if you had told the investigating detective ten years ago what you told me tonight, Henry Silva would be alive today. You're an actress, Jane. You are not a chief of police. You don't get to decide what the cops investigate and what they don't."

"I said I'm sorry. Do I need to say it again?"

"No. Do you happen to know where Bella was on the night of the gala? Had she been invited?"

She took a long, deep breath through her nose. "She was invited to the main event, not the private party, obviously. But she didn't go."

"Why not?"

"She had taken a couple of weeks' vacation. She didn't say where she was going. Everyone was teasing her that she was going to hook up with a girlfriend. In retrospect, Kate was among her main teasers."

"What motive—" I sighed and shook my head. "If everything you are saying is true, what motive would Bella have for killing Kate?"

She stared me in the face. "It's what I am trying to tell you, John. None! You are barking up the wrong tree!"

SIXTEEN

She left me in the lobby without saying goodbye but asked the guy on reception to get Bella for me. She came out ten minutes later frowning, jerked her chin at me, and said, "S'happenin'?"

"Let's go get some coffee."

Her frown became irritable. "I got work."

I fought down my own irritation. "I have a double murder. We can have coffee or I can take you to the 43rd. Your choice."

She sighed and turned to the guy on reception. "Tell Dan I got abducted by aliens, will you." To me, she said, "How long is this going to take?"

This time, I lost the fight. "I don't know, Bella. It's a double homicide investigation! Half an hour? A couple of days? I don't know!"

She turned back to the receptionist. "Half an hour. If it drags on, I'll call."

We found a coffee shop a block away on 9th Avenue. We

got a quiet table and ordered coffee. I had a double espresso, but she ordered an elaborate thing with lots of froth and a heart.

When she'd finished putting sugar in it and stirring it, I said,

"Tell me about your relationship with Katy Hagan."

"This again?"

"When did it start?"

She sighed and watched her spoon as she pulled it out of the foam. She put it in her mouth, sucked it clean, and set it in her saucer.

"This is what you're going to pull me in for? Because somebody told you there was a rumor I was bangin' Kate? Take a hike."

I reached out and pointed at the spoon. "May I?"

"Sure. Knock yourself out."

I took the spoon, pulled a plastic evidence bag from my pocket, and slipped the spoon into it. She watched me as I dropped the spoon into my pocket.

"No, Bill, I am not going to take you in because there is a rumor you were banging Katy Hagan. I am going to pull you in because the skin on the electrical cable that was used to strangle Henry Silva is going to be a match for yours. Because the car I saw at his house the morning he was killed is a match for yours, and because the hair recovered at the scene will also be a match for yours. Now you want to talk to me and tell me why I am wrong, or you want to talk to a lawyer and have her advise you to plea bargain?"

"Son of a bitch."

"Talk to me. I haven't taken you in, and I haven't sent a

car to get you so all your colleagues can watch you being cuffed and arrested. I want to hear what you have to tell me."

"Jeez, boss, I am so grateful."

"Are we done? Or you want to keep pushing? You choose." She stared at me across the table. I said, "Okay, let's start with where you were the morning Silva was killed."

She went to speak but hesitated, then said, "I had the day off. I drank too much the night before, so I stayed in bed late."

"Can anybody vouch for that?"

"No."

"Who were you drinking with the night before?"

"Nobody. I'm a butch forty-year-old transgender dyke. Nobody wants to drink with me."

"You want to tell me how your car got to be at Silva's house that morning?"

She gave a small laugh and leaned back. "What, you memorized my license plate? Or did you just see the most popular car in America parked in his drive, and you assumed it must be the bull dyke's?"

"Bella, I am giving you a chance here. The lab will have processed this DNA in less than twenty-four hours. If it's a match with Silva's killers, everything will be off the table."

"Yeah? So what's on the table right now? Confess to a murder I didn't commit and I get fifteen years instead of twenty?"

I leaned forward with my elbows either side of the espresso and stared her hard in the eye.

"If that's true and you didn't kill Silva, then you have nothing to worry about because the sample will clear you. All I am trying to do is find who killed him and who killed

Kate. Surely you want the same thing! Help me! If you did it, we have you, and it can only help you if you cooperate. If you didn't, then you have nothing to lose and every reason to talk to me."

She spoke with absolutely no expression on her face.

"Such a nice guy. So reasonable, civilized, and mannerly. Hell, you could be a white Obama. Only trouble is, gee whiz, I know you fabricate evidence, and I just *know* a nice guy like you is gonna *hate* a nasty, twisted pervert like me."

I narrowed my eyes at her. "Even if that were true, which it's not, I would rather catch the real killer than put away an innocent nasty pervert like you. Now I am going to tell you what I personally believe right now."

"I can't wait."

"I believe there came a point when you and Kate began to have feelings for each other. You were both loners, you both had a secret, and both of you had the feeling you didn't exactly fit with the people around you."

"My goodness, Dr. Stone, how do you come by these insights?"

I ignored her and went on. "I believe you started a sexual, romantic relationship which you managed to keep hidden from the rest of the crew. Almost."

"Oh, someone spotted us making out by the bike shed and grassed on us?"

"Somebody realized you were becoming close. I believe word got to either Silva or Danny Santos or both. For some reason, they wanted the relationship to end. It might be that they had feelings for her themselves."

"What a siren she was, men and women flocked to her and fell at her feet."

"Or she told them she was through with working as Jane Morley's slave and wanted to make a life of her own. I believe she demanded a large payoff and threatened to write her memoirs and tell the truth about America's sweethearts. That was something they could not allow to happen. Either Silva or Danny Santos went there that night and killed her. Then they provided each other with an alibi."

"Boy, you got some imagination, Detective Stone. You should write books."

"When we reopened the investigation, you heard via Jane that Silva and Danny Santos' alibi wasn't worth a damn, and you went and killed Silva. For some reason, you thought he was the most likely of the two."

"You're full of shit, Stone. You done? I have a job to get back to."

"If you're innocent of these murders, Bella, why won't you talk to me?"

"I just told you. You're full of shit."

"So put me straight. Who killed Kate?"

"You think I know? You think if I knew I wouldn't have—"

I waited a beat and asked, "What? Wouldn't have what?"

She took a deep breath.

"You think I wouldn't have told the investigating officers at the time?"

I shook my head.

"No, I don't think you would have. With your view of the cops, that we are corrupt and manufacture evidence? If you suspected powerful, influential people like Silva, and especially Danny Santos, who were providing each other with alibis, I think you would have kept your mouth shut and your profile low. Especially as that little clique were the only ones who knew your particular secret."

She leaned across the table. "I did not kill Silva, and I don't believe he killed Kate. He was way too smart and had a hundred more effective ways to destroy a person. Neither do I believe Danny Boy has the balls to kill anyone. If he had, he'd have killed his wife years ago. So who's your remaining suspect? Me? Maybe with your fantastic imagination, you can tell me why, being helplessly in love with Kate, I decided to kill her."

"Did you? Maybe she was going to tell the whole damned world you were a man. She had repressed her lesbianism all her life. She fell for you, and that distressed her because it was proof of what she didn't want to believe. But when she discovered you were really a man, she felt saved, liberated from sin, and wanted to tell everybody."

I had chosen my words carefully, stressing that she was in reality a man, and that she might think what they were doing was a sin. I wanted to see if it provoked violent anger in her. She stared at me for a long moment. Her pupils were pinpricks, and I could see a muscle bunching in her jaw.

"Good luck with your DNA samples, Detective Stone. I hope you catch whoever did this. Kate was a good person, I was fond of her, and Silva was a good friend to Jane. Goodbye."

She stood and walked out.

I finished my espresso and went out to my car. There I called Dehan.

"Stone, where are you?"

"At the studio on Upper West Side. I'm going to take Joe a teaspoon. You want to come along?"

"Yeah. I'm going crazy locked in here. I made sourdough bread. You like sourdough bread? I was thinking maybe I could paint the kitchen. You think pink is a nice color for the kitchen? It might be a boy. I could paint it blue."

"I'm on my way."

We arrived at the lab at midday, and I handed Joe the spoon.

"I need to know if this is the same DNA as the skin on the cable, the saliva on Silva's face, the glass, and the hair. I need it ASAP, Joe. I have a bad feeling somebody else is going to get hurt if we don't nail this guy soon."

He took the spoon, handed it to a technician, and gave him instructions. When he came back, he put his hand on my shoulder and guided us toward his office. It was somewhat larger and more orderly than Frank's, with heavy, minimalist Scandinavian furniture and views over the gardens that flank Seminole Avenue.

"On that subject, there are a couple of things I wanted to discuss with you and Carmen about those letters."

He seated us at his desk and pulled a file from a cabinet. He dropped it on the desk and sat in a large, brown leather chair. He opened the file, and I saw the letters inside it, each in a sealed, plastic sleeve. There were also several printed pages which he picked up and scanned.

"The typewriter is a pretty old portable Olivetti." He gave his head a small shake. "I mean maybe fifty or sixty years. But that is not the most interesting thing. Two features really stand out. I've had them examined independently by a forensic linguist and a psychologist, and they both agreed, independently, that the letters seem to be written by two different people."

I grunted, and Dehan glanced at me. "That's what you said."

"Could they be written by a person with a split personality?"

He nodded several times. "That's what I asked the forensic psychologist. He said it was impossible to tell, but it was certainly a possibility. So I went the extra nine yards and posed the question I imagined you would want to ask."

Dehan interrupted, "Could a switch from personality A to Personality B be accompanied by a serious increase in physical strength?"

"Right. Because from what you told me, the guy who wrote these letters was not exactly King Kong."

I said, "What did he say?"

"It is a phenomenon which has been known to happen quite frequently, both with artificial stimulation through drugs, but also in states of rage or extreme aggression. However, as you know, in order to stand up in court, you would have to have the accused psychiatrically assessed."

"Okay, that's interesting. And the other thing? I'm guessing you're saving the best for last."

"Yeah, it's a bit odd. Bob Newport's prints were on the envelopes, right? He clearly made no effort to hide them either because, like most people, he didn't realize paper holds a print or because he didn't care."

"Okay."

He squinted at me, smiled, and shook his head. "But the letters don't have his prints on them. They have somebody else's prints."

Dehan frowned and sat forward. "You're kidding."

"Nope. This person is not on IAFIS. Apparently they have no record. And the prints are small. It's a person with small, delicate fingers."

Dehan said, "A man?"

"It could be. It's impossible to say. A pianist, a classical guitarist, someone with fine, delicate hands."

Dehan turned to me. "It goes back to what we said in the beginning, Stone. He's writing them but then getting somebody else to address them and send them. He's just making sure not to touch the letters."

Joe shook his head. "That doesn't make sense. *His* prints are on the envelope. That would make him the person who posted them. But he's admitted to you that he wrote them. It's like he had somebody feeding the paper into the typewriter while he typed."

I sighed. "That's just bizarre. And these prints are on the letters that are plain fan mail *and* the ones that become aggressive?"

"Yup. Every single one of them."

I was frowning hard, feeling the answer was almost within reach but still unable to see it. "The prints that are on the letters, the small, delicate ones, are they on the envelopes too?"

"Oh yes. Not so much, but they do appear on the envelopes."

Dehan did that thing with the shrugging, spreading hands, and shaking head all at the same time. "Then it's a friend of his. Somebody he hangs out with. They did it together."

Joe shrugged. "Maybe. That part is your job. Unfortunately, it leaves the question unanswered, did he, or they, kill Kate Hagan?"

"What about Silva?" I said. "Did he—or they—kill Silva? Did you get any prints from the glass? The one that had lipstick on it?"

He leaned back in his chair and made a small grimace. "That was weird," he said. "There was lipstick and saliva on it. But the glass had been wiped."

Dehan said, "That doesn't make sense."

He raised his shoulder slightly. "People watch these crime procedurals, and they get weird ideas about forensics. They think glass holds a print and paper doesn't, and they get the idea that lipstick and whiskey will remove DNA. That's all I can think."

We talked for another ten minutes but got no closer to an explanation. Finally, he promised us he'd get the DNA profile results to us as soon as they were available, and we thanked him and left to go and hunt down some lunch.

SEVENTEEN

We had eaten our lunch in silence and now sat at Emilio's Pizza staring at a double espresso and a green tea. Dehan, as so often, was the first to speak.

"We are right back where we started."

I glanced at her, was quiet for a moment, then said, "Not quite. Almost, but not quite."

"No?" She looked skeptical. "Enlighten me. From where I'm sitting, we have described a huge circle and come right back to where we started."

I held up one finger. "One important thing has changed. If we could find a match for those new, small fingerprints at Silva's house, it would suggest very strongly that whoever killed Silva also killed Kate and had some connection with Bob Newport. It would start to tie this all together."

She raised her eyebrows and pushed out her bottom lip, then gave a slow shrug.

"I guess, but why would you think we might? Joe already told us the prints on the glass had been wiped."

"He did." I sipped my coffee and set it carefully in the saucer again. "But I am thinking."

"Thinking what?"

I gave a small sigh. "I knew there was something about Silva's den which troubled me. I couldn't place it, but it was nagging at the back of my mind. Then I realized, I couldn't place what was troubling me because I was focusing on the room as an office or a study. But it wasn't an office thing that was wrong. And of course we didn't know when we looked over the place that he and his killer had been drinking whiskey. So why would we notice a whiskey bottle or a decanter or a tray of drinks…?"

I left the words hanging and watched her face. It became abstracted as her eyes strayed to the wall opposite and lost focus. Finally she gave her head a little shake.

"There was no bottle of whiskey, no decanter, not even a tray."

"Right, and when Joe told us there was lipstick on the glass, it started nagging at the back of my mind. Something was wrong. What was wrong was that there was no drinks try, no bar, nothing. So maybe Silva didn't drink in his den, but a guy like him, he'd have a drinks tray." I drummed a little tattoo with my fingers. "I disturbed the killer when he was about to wash the glasses, but maybe he was doing more than that. Maybe he was trying to remove all trace of the drinks, all trace that Silva knew his killer."

She frowned at me. "So…?"

"So that house has a cellar. Did you notice the small windows at ground level?"

"Sure, that's probably where the boiler is."

"Right, and with a man like Silva, it might be where he keeps his wine and his spirits."

She thought about it. "That's a hell of a reach, Sensei."

I gave my eyebrows and my shoulders a fractional hitch. "Maybe. And if not in the cellar, somewhere else. But you have to ask, right? Where is the whiskey they were drinking?"

She thought about it some more and finally said, "Right—right? And if it came from a bottle, there's a chance he left some prints on it. So let's go have a look."

We took a small detour via a return visit to Joe's lab and made it to Riverdale by three o'clock that afternoon. The yellow tape was still draped across the entrance, shifting slightly in the breeze. Dehan got out to remove it, and I pulled in where I had parked before, behind the Mercedes Benz. I climbed out, and Dehan reached in the back for a shoulder bag Joe had lent us while I opened the door to the house.

The irregular shaped entrance hall was dark but for a slab of sunlight that lay across the tiled floor. The house was still, and the silence was like a physical presence. Dehan came up behind me, casting a long shadow across the floor in front of me. She stopped, and together we listened to the emptiness.

"They took the body," she said, speaking half to herself, "but they left the death behind."

I glanced at her over my shoulder. "You want to wait outside?"

"Nah." She shook her head. "I'm grateful to this bozo. He could have killed you but he left you alive instead. I owe him."

I frowned at the art deco doors, remembering the painful blow to my head and waking up face down on the stairs. "Yeah, I noticed that too. I wonder why he did it." I pointed to the doors. "You reckon the entrance to the cellar is in the kitchen?"

"Reckon so."

The kitchen was large, with a pine table in the center of a terracotta floor. It was the only concession there was to organic materials. Everything else was sparkling chrome, steel, or plastic. It looked more like a laboratory than a place where cooking might happen.

There was a door beside the sink that opened onto a lawn, a large herb garden, and an orchard. It had red and white gingham curtains over a pane of glass, where fall light filtered in. Opposite that door, there was another which had a small brass plaque with the word *Hemer* inscribed on it. Dehan smiled.

"Cute."

"It is?"

"*Hemer*, it's Hebrew. It is the blood of the grape but also conveys the idea of foaming and boiling. I think, so far at least, your hunch is right. It's the boiler and the wine cellar."

"Clever me."

I opened the door, and a light came on automatically overhead, revealing a broad staircase tiled in terracotta with a pine handrail on the right. I went down with Dehan just behind me. At the bottom, we found that on the right, the room opened out into a kind of junk area full of old sofas, cartons of books, and toys and broken chairs. There was a large boiler in the center, and to the left, there was a short passage which led to another door and the wine cellar I had known would be there.

It was cool, insulated from the boiler room, with wine racks floor to ceiling, maybe ten feet tall or more. Over to one side, there was a dusty antique credenza, and in front of it an ancient, mahogany table with six chairs set around it.

Dehan pointed to the wall on her left. Her voice was startling in the insulated silence.

"These are red wines. The racks are labeled Bordeaux, the next two are burgundy. These are white Bordeaux, white burgundy, wine, wine, wine…"

I moved to the opposite side of the room.

"These are fortified wines, sherry, port, Madeira. These are spirits. Cognac, Armagnac…"

Dehan's voice came to me. "New World wines, Australia, New Zealand, California…"

I stopped. "Ah, okay, Scotch, Irish, Canadian… As far as I can see, all the bottles are sealed—"

Dehan's voice cut across me. "Stone, what's that on the black barrel in the corner?"

I turned and squinted. The corner was in deep shadow, and the barrel was black, so it was almost invisible. But sitting on the top of it, like it was a table, was a silver tray. On the tray, there were a couple of decanters, four crystal tumblers, and a bottle of the Macallan.

She crossed the room, pulling a pair of latex gloves from her pocket, and hunkered down beside the bottle, pulling on the gloves.

"It's been opened. There are more than two measures missing." She frowned. "I guess it was in his study and he'd had a couple of shots." She turned her frown on me. "So the drinks tray *was* in his study. They have a drink while they talk. He wipes his prints from the glasses—why not do the same with the bottle? Why go to the trouble of bringing it down here?"

I pulled out a chair and sat with my elbows on the table and my chin in my hands, staring at the bottle, trying to visualize the scene. It was hard.

"Like I said, maybe the intention was to remove any indication he knew his killer. He'd got as far as bringing the tray down and wiping his prints fro his glass when I turned up."

"He or she, Stone, depending on how you look at it. He or she thought they had time. They didn't expect anyone to show up because they knew Silva had removed himself from the city after we started our investigation.

"So whoever it is drives up to the house, and Silva lets him or her in." She paused and gave her head a small shake. "And I have to tell you, Stone, the more I think this through, the more my money is on Bella for this. She just ticks all the boxes. So they have a talk over a drink. She gets behind him and Tasers him, strangles him, and then sets about removing any trace that Silva knew his killer. Part of that involves washing the glasses and bringing the whisky bottle down to the cellar where it will not be noticed." She pointed to the small windows high on the walls. "But while she's doing that, she hears your car arrive and panics. She runs up the stairs. The other two glasses—it's a set of six, right?—she has left in the kitchen where she planned to wash them. But by the time she gets there, you are already in the house. She waits for you to start up the stairs with your back to her, jumps out, and slugs you."

I thought it through. "That makes a lot of sense. What about the song on repeat?"

"She lost her love. Kate was her Eurydice. In her mind, she was killed by Silva." She gave a small, humorless laugh. "His retreating to his country house after we went to see him must have confirmed her suspicions."

I stared at her face staring back at me and nodded. "Well, let's see. Let's find out. You got the stuff?"

"Yeah. I did a course on this. Let me do it."

She opened the bag and pulled out an aerosol can and a plastic bottle of water. She sprayed the bottle from top to bottom, taking care to cover the cork and both labels. Then, taking great care to touch only areas that were unlikely to be gripped, she doused the bottle with water. After a few seconds, dark prints began to appear on the label and on the clear glass. I went and hunkered down beside her, and we slowly and methodically examined each print. After a moment, I pointed at the rear label.

"There, and"—I peered around the other side at the front label—"there, a thumb and a middle finger, like the bottle was picked up with just thumb and finger"—I demonstrated, holding my hand like a pair of pliers—"to take it off or put it on the tray. They are slim, narrow, not like the other prints on the bottle."

Dehan pointed to the glass beside the label. "That's probably Silva's thumb." She carefully spun the bottle. "See on the other side? There, forefinger, middle, and ring. That's his pinky. He's gripped the bottle in his hand to pour. They are totally different than the ones on the label. This bozo doesn't know paper holds a print. You'd better take some photographs and send them to Joe. I'll bag the bottle."

I took the pictures, sent them, and called Joe.

"John, I'm just opening the pictures. Any luck?"

"Maybe. They look similar. Let me know as soon as you've made the comparison, will you?"

"You've got it. Ten, fifteen minutes."

"Joe, if they are a match, it might mean the killer was down here in the cellar. You better have some guys come and look around."

"I'll call you back in ten."

We made our way up to the kitchen and out to the car. Dehan leaned her back against the trunk, and I stood and stared up at the fresh, blue sky. There was a small, chill breeze and one small cloud taking its time headed west.

Dehan, not for the first or last time, spoke my thoughts.

"If the prints are a match, it means the same person who put the letters in the envelopes handled the bottle of whiskey."

"Yes," I told the cloud.

"Okay, baby steps. So *that* means the person who handled the letters—not necessarily the person who wrote them, Bob—was at the scene of the Silva murder. Can we take that step?"

"Yes."

"But it does not place that person at Kate's murder."

"No, but indirectly it links him or her to it."

She frowned down at her boots. "It links him or her to it because she touched the letters Bob Newport sent to Jane and Kate stashed away. That's pretty indirect."

"And yet it is too much of a coincidence to ignore it."

She nodded at her boots. "Agreed, but Stone, I have no idea what it means."

I took a couple of steps toward her with my hands thrust in my pockets. "It means that whoever handled the letters killed Silva and Kate. What we don't know is what the motivation was or who owns those prints, but that person killed both victims."

She shook her head. "That is speculation, Stone. All it proves is that one person handled the whiskey bottle and the letters. That is all it proves."

I nodded. "Correct. And not the envelopes, just the letters. That is all it proves, Little Grasshopper. But what it *means* is that the same person who handled those letters killed Kate and Silva. Mark my words."

Before she could answer, my cell rang.

"Joe, what have you got?" I put it on speaker.

"John. I can tell you that the person who held that bottle of Macallan with such care by the label also handled those letters with the same kind of care. I think Dehan is right; this person thinks paper won't hold a print. Actually, you were lucky. That spray I gave you doesn't work on porous surfaces, but most glass bottle labels these days are made of plastic films like polyester, polypropylene, and more often, biaxially oriented polypropylene."

"That's the kind of lucky guy I am."

"I'll get back to you as soon as I get a result on the spoon."

We stared at each other a moment. Then she said, "What are Bella's hands like? I'm trying to visualize them."

I gave a small shrug. "They are not as manly as you might expect. She's quite small."

"Could they be hers?"

I shook my head. "I don't know, Dehan. They could be,

I guess. If we get a hit on the spoon, we'll book her and get our answer."

She gave me a funny smile. "You like her, don't you?"

"No." I shrugged again. "She's tried so hard to find herself and, quite literally, recreate herself. It would be a shame if she has blown all that. I guess I'd like to believe that at heart she's a good person. But we just don't know yet."

"Okay, so what now?"

I looked up at the sky again. The cloud was gone, well on its way to California. What now?

"You know what I want to do?" I looked down at her. "I want to talk to Bob Newport again. I want to know where his poems are."

"You do? You want to tell me why?"

I nodded. "Mm-hmm. I'll tell you in the car. Let's get back to the station."

EIGHTEEN

Dehan had called Bob Newport on the way to the station. Now we were sitting at our desks in the detectives' room waiting for him. Dehan was looking at her boots, which were crossed on the corner of the desk, and I was staring at the cold sky through the window. Neither of us had spoken. Now Dehan said, "Stone?"

"Mm-hmm?"

"Have we been—are we being really stupid?"

"I think so."

"I mean, Bella is a guy, right? I mean, operation and hormones aside, she's a guy. She's short, but she's butch, strong, like a guy."

I had shifted my attention from the sky to Dehan. "I get it."

"I don't think her hands *would* make such small prints. So—" She took her feet off the desk and sat forward, with her elbows on her knees. "So what if we've been running the wild goose chase to end all wild goose chases?"

"I think we have, but what's on your mind?"

"Jane came to us in the beginning with those letters, and that is the reason we took the case. It was the damn letters that started this whole new investigation. And the first thing we do is look at them and discard them! So that we can go galloping off chasing after suspects who had been cleared already in the first investigation!"

"Wrongly cleared, Dehan, because their alibis were false."

"Yeah, okay, but hear me out, Stone. Let's say that Kate and Bella did, as Jane said, start getting feelings for each other. Let's say that, when the big gala comes up, as two members who were devoted to Jane but unwelcome at the party, they decide to book a hotel room and spend a day or two together. Kate goes and settles into the room first, and for some reason Bella has things to see to, whatever, and has to arrive later."

"She was off sick, remember?"

"Right, well, maybe she had to see the doc. Who knows? Right now, the important thing is that Kate is alone in the room. Now granted that they lied about their alibi to keep themselves out of trouble, but let's say their motive for lying was not to hide their guilt, but to avoid negative publicity. And the truth was not so far from what they said. Jane was with Simon, the aspiring actor, Danny was with his two unconscious hookers, according to his—"

"Don't say it."

"Proclivity, and Silva was passed out on the other hooker's bosom while she watched TV."

"So...?"

"And our boy, who *did* write those damned letters, and

who does have small, delicate hands, *had* developed an obsessive fixation, but not with Jane, America's sweetheart—with Kate. He came to see her and Silva as the evil creatures who were standing between him and Jane, his soul mate, the love of his life. Exactly as we thought right from the start."

"So how come—"

"I know exactly what you're going to say. How come once Kate was dead he stopped writing? But, my dear Watson, I have already explained that. His true fixation had shifted from Jane to Kate. Once she was dead, he lost interest in Jane."

"Bob was in the system, remember?"

"Exactly, for sexual misdemeanors."

"But his prints were on the envelope. The ones on the letters were not his."

She waved a dismissive hand at me. "How hard would it be, Stone, to get a couple of prints in a piece of silicon? A pair of surgical gloves worn by a petite nurse, 'Can you hold this please?' There must be a thousand and one ways for a resourceful nerd to get a couple of small fingerprints that he can impress on a letter."

"And ten years later on a bottle of Macallan?"

"Why not? All he needs is two things: palms that sweat when he's nervous, and a disposition common in weird freaks who kill people: the inclination to keep trophies from his killings."

I sighed and rubbed my face. "So you're saying his fixation shifted, and he started to stalk Kate, followed her to the hotel. She let him in for some reason—"

"Maybe he said he was hotel staff with something for the room."

"He kills her. And all the letters he has sent Jane he has deliberately imprinted with fake, misleading fingerprints. But not the envelopes. He has done this in order to create a red herring, because he knows he is going to kill her in the future. The problem is, he *doesn't* know yet that he's going to kill her. We discussed that already."

She scowled at me. "So maybe he does. Maybe he knew from the start, but as time went by, like I said, the object of his obsession changed, and he killed Kate instead." She threw up her hands in exasperation. "Stone, the prints are *on his letters!*"

I groaned. "So why the hell did he kill Silva?"

She snapped her fingers and pointed at me. "Because he is on a quest to free Jane! Remember he told us Kate and Silva wanted to stop her from becoming free. Her agent and her PA had her imprisoned and were keeping her from him."

"Why did he wait ten years for the second hit?"

She sighed and sagged back into her chair. "I don't know. It had something to do with us taking the investigation. Can *you* do any better? One hard, solid, immovable fact stands out above all the mess and chaos, Stone. The small, narrow prints were on the letters he wrote. So either he faked them or he had an accomplice. It's that simple."

I grunted, but before I could say anything more incisive than "Ungh," Maria, the desk sergeant, poked her head around the door and told us Bob Newport had been taken up to Interrogation Room Three. We grabbed the file with his letters, and three paper cups of dirty black water from the machine and climbed the stairs.

He was not sitting when we went in. He was standing with his hands behind his back, scrutinizing the one-way mirror that separated him from the observation room. He glanced at us.

"Is there anyone in there, watching me?"

"Not today." I put the coffee on the table. "I need to ask you, Mr. Newport. This interview is being filmed and recorded. Do you object to that?"

He was still staring into the mirror. "No."

"Do you play piano, Mr. Newport?"

He turned to look at me, with his hands behind his back. "Why do you ask?"

Dehan had sat. I gestured to the chair across the table. "Please, take a seat. Your hands, they look like a musician's hands."

He didn't look at them. He walked around the table and sat. "I am not a musician, Detective Stone."

"But you are a poet."

"I am a very poor poet. I don't mean that I am financially poor, though I am, but that my poetry is poor, mawkish, and overly sentimental, as I am sure you already know. However, bad poetry is not a crime, I believe, though perhaps it should be." His eyes shifted to Dehan. "You really are excessively beautiful, Detective Dehan."

"Let's stay on task, Mr. Newport —"

"What *is* the task, Detective Stone?"

I opened the file with his letters in it. Each was contained in a clear, plastic sleeve with its corresponding envelope in the bottom right corner. I placed my hand on the top one.

"I have read each and every one of these letters several times over. Where are the poems? You said you sent her poems. Where are they?"

He stared for a long time at the folder, then shifted his

gaze to my face. He blinked just once and returned his gaze to the stack of letters.

"Is this some kind of trap?"

Dehan frowned. "What are you talking about?"

"You're planting evidence to frame me."

I didn't answer. Dehan said again, "What are you talking about, Bob?"

He pointed across the table at the file. "Those envelopes. Those are my envelopes, but those are not my letters. I will deny it, and you cannot prove that I wrote them."

I said, "Relax, nobody is trying to frame you, Bob. We are just trying to understand what has happened here." I took the top letter out. It was the first one he'd written to Jane. I handed it to him. "Did you write this?"

He shook his head. "No."

"Just take it and read it and tell me if they are your words."

He hesitated, then took it and read the first paragraph.

"What is this?" He looked up at me. "What the hell is this?"

"You tell me, Bob."

"These are my words. This is the first letter I ever wrote to Jane Morley."

I leafed through the letters in front of me until I came to the fifth, and I handed him that.

"Are these your words?"

He read through it and looked up at me again. "You want to tell me what's going on, Detective Stone? Am I being accused of something? What is this?"

"You are not being accused of anything. Please answer the question. Are those your words?"

"Yes, but I did not write this letter."

Dehan was frowning at me but trying hard to hide it. I leafed through the letters again until I came to the tenth, after the tone of the letters had changed and started becoming more aggressive. I handed it to him. "What about this one?"

Before he'd gotten three lines in, he was shaking his head emphatically. "No, absolutely not. This is just absolutely not my style, and I would never address that beautiful woman in this way. And besides—"

"Before you go on, Bob, you said you had sent Jane Morley some poems. How many exactly?"

"My God! It's ten years ago! Maybe three?"

"You still have copies of them?"

"Somewhere."

"They are not among these letters." I took the last five and spread them out in front of him. "Will you look at these and tell me if they are your words?"

It didn't take him long. He scanned through them, shaking his head ever more emphatically. "These are *not* my letters. I did *not* write them. The first ones were my words, though I did not write them. But these—" He waved his hand at them. "These have absolutely nothing to do with me. I mean"—he gestured at them again with both hands—"surely even you can see that the style is totally different. I'd have to have a split personality or something."

"Bob, I am going to ask you a question, and I need you to be very clear and precise. How do you know so emphatically, how can you be so sure, that these are not the letters you wrote?"

"Because in the first place I can't type, and in the second

place, I don't own a typewriter. I write all my letters in longhand. It is the *only* way to write a letter! Furthermore, why on Earth would I sign off with that absurd signature, 'Your Man'? I mean, please! Aside from being impossibly presumptuous, what is wrong with Bob Newport? Or if we became more intimate, Bob?"

He looked at us both in turn like there was something wrong with us for not seeing what was patently obvious. Dehan leaned her elbows on the table and studied his face a moment.

"Mr. Newport, what made you stop writing to Jane Morley?"

He sighed heavily and shook his head.

"It was a number of things, really. I had been growing rather bored of the one-way correspondence, to be perfectly honest. I write to a lot of people from all walks of life, and I have to say I have struck up some very lively, interesting dialogues. But, honestly, after ten or fifteen letters, or whatever it was, I started getting bored. The penny had dropped that she was never going to answer, probably because her PA and her agent didn't want her straying outside of their control, and then of course her personal assistant was murdered. So I thought it was probably time to move on."

He looked down at the letters in front of him and gave a sudden, astonished laugh.

"But seeing these, my goodness! You must have thought *I* had killed her!"

"We did." It was Dehan. "And it's still a possibility. You have a record of sexual offenses, Mr. Newport. And we only have your word for the fact that you didn't write those letters."

If she thought she was going to scare him or shake him up, she was wrong. He rolled his eyes, pulled a pen from his inside pocket, and reached a hand across the table to her.

"Piece of paper please!"

She pulled a piece from her notebook and slid it across the table to him. To me he said, "May I see one of those envelopes, please?"

I spun the folder so he could see it. Carefully, but without hesitation, he wrote out the address on the envelope. When he was done, he put the pen away and handed me the sheet of paper.

"I am not a fool now, and I was not a fool ten years ago. I know perfectly well that handwriting is almost as compelling as a fingerprint when it comes to identifying someone." He jabbed a finger at the folder. "That address and the one I have just penned were written by the same person. Now you tell me, if I had a typewriter with which to type an anonymous letter, why in the name of all that is sacred would I handwrite the address? Why not just type it? The answer, Detectives, is that I handwrote the letters. I have another question for you. You may have noticed that in the first two or three letters, I asked her a number of questions about her tastes and habits."

He paused. It was hard not to react, but I had Dehan's words from earlier ringing in my ears: *Have we been—are we being really stupid?* I said, "How was she intended to answer those questions?"

"Precisely. If I am anonymous, and there is no return address, how is she expected to answer? Well, again, the answer, Detectives, is that I included my address in the letter heading, as any well-brought-up person does. Or did, at least."

I sighed. "We are almost done, Bob."

"Forgive me for interrupting, Detective Stone, but could you explain to me why I am Bob to you, but you are Detective Stone to me? I don't think actually that we are on cordial, intimate terms, especially as you seem to have attempted to frame me for murder. Could you perhaps address me as Mr. Newport, as your colleague does?"

"Of course, Mr. Newport. I have just one more question for you. Where were you on the morning of—"

"The morning Henry Silva was killed. You really are priceless."

"Where were you, Mr. Newport?"

"I was at choir practice, Detective Stone! My grandparents were Welsh, and we have a strong choral tradition." He grabbed his pen from his pocket and scrawled an address and a telephone number on the paper Dehan had given him earlier. "Inconvenient as that is for you, Detectives, I did not kill Katy Hagan, I did not kill Henry Silva, I do not own a typewriter, and I do not drive. In fact, I barely leave my apartment unless it's to go to my local church for choir practice. All I do is write letters to people I find interesting. I do not kill them. May I please leave now?"

I nodded down at the table. "Yes, Mr. Newport, you may leave now."

He stood and marched out of the interrogation room with more dignity than he had left me. When the door had closed behind him, I offered Dehan what you might call a sheepish smile. She laughed and shook her head.

"I guess the answer to your question have we been or are we being really stupid? might be yes."

"Let's not be hard on ourselves, Stone. This is a real brain teaser. I'm about as lost as Little Red Riding Hood in the Amazon jungle. But you—" She pointed at me and frowned. "You already had a hunch he hadn't written those letters. You should have told me."

"Yeah, I know. I just wasn't sure. I needed to test it."

"So what the hell does that mean? Somebody copied his letters? What the hell for?"

"Somebody copied his letters and added a few more because they wanted to frame him for Kate's murder."

She covered her face with her hands, then spread them wide, up at the ceiling, in a plea to God.

"So we are back to Danny or Bella!"

"Eliminate the impossible, and whatever's left, however improbable, is the truth."

"There is just one problem with that, Stone."

"Yup."

"Either everything is impossible, or nothing is impossible."

I nodded. "I agree. But we will hear very shortly that the DNA on Bella's spoon matches the DNA at the scene of Silva's murder. And then we will know."

"You know that?"

"I think so."

NINETEEN

We walked slowly down to the detectives' room. Halfway down, I stopped. Dehan went on a few steps, then turned and came back.

"What?"

"How did Bella get ahold of those letters?"

"I have no idea."

"She had to got ahold of the letters, copy the first few onto an Olivetti typewriter, create a few more of her own, and somehow get into Danny and Jane's house and plant them. Not just that, but plant them where Kate would have put them."

I took another couple of steps with Dehan one step behind me. Then I stopped again. She collided with me, gently taking hold of my arm.

"That," I said, raising a finger, "is very meticulous, careful planning."

"That's not out of character in Bella. She seems to have

had everything planned out from when she was a boy." Then she added, "Maybe Kate got her the letters."

"What would be her purpose in doing that?"

"I don't know, Stone. I honestly feel beat. I don't remember a case as confusing as this one."

"Kate acquires the letters that will be used by her lover to implicate an innocent man in her own murder."

We reached the lobby, and I moved out onto the steps that led down to the sidewalk. There I stopped and stared up over the trees at where the blue sky was turning golden in the dying light of the sun.

"Incongruous," I told Dehan. "The whole thing is incongruous. You get three things that seem to work together, and then a fourth makes it impossible. Two other things make sense together, but a third contradicts them. The whole, damn thing is..."—I shook my head at the sky—"just *that!* Incongruous."

She came and stood beside me, looking up at the sky too. "Is that like your proclivity word? For you it's incongruous?"

I went cold. I felt my hair stir and prickle on my head. I said quietly, "An incongruous proclivity, Dehan." I laughed at the obviousness of it, and at how stupid I had been to miss it. "An incongruous proclivity."

"Care to explain?"

But before I could, my cell rang.

"Yeah, Stone."

"Hi, John, it's Joe here, from the lab. I'm sending you the report, but I thought you'd like to know right away. The DNA on the spoon is a match for the saliva on Silva's face and the skin on the cable that was used to strangle him.

Whoever spat on that guy and held that cable, that's your guy."

I was quiet for a moment. Then, "Thanks, Joe. Take it easy. Have a good evening."

I hung up and stood staring at the black screen. Dehan went up and down on her toes a couple of times.

"So what did he say?"

"Bella's DNA is a match for the saliva on Silva's face and the skin on the electrical cable. Bella's the guy."

She gave a small wince. "I guess that was obvious from the start. We just didn't see it clearly. But in retrospect, it was always going to be her. We need a search warrant for her house. We need that typewriter."

"Yes," I said and nodded slowly for a while as the gold slowly drained from the sky. "I guess it was always going to be her."

We arrived at West 57th Street with the sun hovering over Brooklyn, hiding behind the Central Park Tower among the canyons of steel and glass. We had a patrol car with us, but I told them to wait at the corner of 10th Avenue, outside the Coughy Shop. I'd call them if I needed them. I'd asked Dehan to wait at the station, but she said the chances of Bella turning violent at the studio were minimal, plus we had the uniforms in the car. I didn't like it, but neither did I have much choice.

Now we climbed out of the Jag and made our way up the steps and into the lobby. I reached for my badge, but the guy on reception gave an ironic smile and said, "I knows who y'are. Who'd j'want?"

I nodded at him. "Thanks. I'm looking for Bella Milano, the gaffer."

He shook his head. "She ain't here. She ain't come back since you talked to her last. But Miss Morley said if you showed up again to call her. She wants to talk with yiz."

I glanced at Dehan. She shrugged. I said, "Okay, let her know we're here."

"I already did."

A moment later, the door to the studios opened, and Jane rushed out.

"John"—she glanced at Dehan—"Carmen"—back to me. "What's happening?"

Dehan arched an eyebrow. "What are you talking about?"

"Bella!" She stared hard at Dehan, her eyes flitting over her face. "Bella," she said again.

I said, "What about Bella, Jane?"

"You came for her this morning, now she's gone. Tell me you haven't—"

"Pipe down, Jane! I didn't come for her this morning. I came to talk to her. It's what cops do. She didn't feel great after we'd talked, so maybe she went home." I could feel Dehan eyeing me with a curious frown. I turned to the guy at the desk. "Has she called in?"

He shook his head. Jane said, "So you're not here to…"

"We're here to do our jobs, Jane. If you hear from Bella, let me know. We need to talk to her."

I turned to go, but her voice stopped me. "John!" I paused and looked at her. "She called me."

"Where is she?"

"She's at home. She said she was terrified you were trying

to frame her. She was half hysterical saying that the cops were all homophobic and you were going to plant evidence. I told her to calm down, that you weren't like that." Her eyes flitted to Dehan for just a moment, then back to me. "That you were a good man."

"Thanks."

"She said she was going to Mexico. I told her not to be a fool." She hesitated. "John, is she...?"

I didn't answer her. It didn't seem to me to be a conversation worth having. I pushed out of the door and moved quickly to the car. Dehan climbed in the other side, and we slammed the doors. I turned the key and covered the sixty yards to the uniforms in the patrol car all in slightly less than five seconds. Dehan leaned out of the window and told them, "Turneur Avenue, bottom of Castle Hill Avenue."

I leaned across her. "You'll get there ahead of us. No sirens. You wait at a distance, fifty, sixty yards. Wait for us. Only move in if you see her leaving."

The driver gave me the thumbs-up. They made a U-turn around my trunk and took off with their sirens blaring at the intersection. We followed. Dehan was staring at me.

"They'll get there before us? This growler is old, but it's fast."

"I'm taking you to the station first. She's panicking and might be—"

"No way, Stone! Don't even dream about it."

"It is not open for discussion."

"Bullshit! We have two uniforms there and you. We proceed with caution. You *cannot* cut me out of the arrest! No way, Stone. I'll get emotional! I won't speak to you till the kid is ten years old! I swear, Stone! If he's a boy, I'll make him wear pink shirts and a bow tie! I'm *serious!*"

"Dehan!"

"I won't get out of the car. You'll have to manhandle me." She waved a finger at me. "I am dangerous when I am mad. You won't make the arrest and she'll get away!"

"Fine! But you stay in the car, and you let me and Weller and Joyce make the arrest."

She grinned. "Right, sure." And then, "There will be no trouble, Stone. She knows she's beat. But I'll keep back."

"Dehan, it's not just you and me—"

"I know! Jeez, you're like my mother."

"That would make me our child's grandmother."

She narrowed her eyes at me but didn't say anything.

By the time we got to Turneur Avenue, the sun had slipped below the horizon, but darkness had not set in yet. Weller and Joyce were parked seventy yards from the house on the far side of the road. The lights were on in the windows, and a white Toyota Corolla was parked outside with the trunk open. It was about a foot from the neighbor's car in front, but it had space behind.

Dehan pointed. "Put it in at an angle across her ass."

I did what she suggested, killed the engine, and pulled the handbrake.

"You stay in the car. I'll let you know when it's safe."

"Yes, Mom."

I ignored her and climbed out. I walked the length of the path across the front yard and came to the open door. All the lights were on inside. and I could hear Maria Callas coming from in back. It was *La Bohème*, "Si Mi Chiamano Mimi."

"Bella?" There was no answer. "Bella, it's Detective Stone, NYPD. I need to talk to you."

I crossed the threshold, oddly aware of the birds singing their evening chorus outside. The door to the front room was open, and the lights were on, but the room was empty. The glass in the bow window was an odd, dusky gray. I moved to the back room. The door was also open. There were three lamps burning on occasional tables. It was a comfortable room with an open fireplace, lots of books.

She was sitting in an old armchair staring at the cold fire. In her hand, she had a crystal tumbler with an inch of whiskey in it. The music was loud. It filled the room with Callas' impossibly beautiful, tragic voice. I leaned on the jamb. She knew I was there, but she didn't look at me. I waited for the song to end.

The room went quiet, and I pushed off the door and went to sit opposite her in the other armchair. Her eyes shifted from the fireplace to take in my face.

Maria Callas had started to sing again, "Un Bel de Vedremo." I reached for the remote control beside the bottle of Johnny Walker on her table.

"Let it finish."

We sat while it swelled to the climax, then faded. I pressed the button, and silence fell.

"You got your DNA results."

"Yes."

"So it's over."

"You want to tell me how it got there?"

Her smile creased her right cheek. "Not really, Stone. You came to arrest me. Do what you gotta do."

"Is it Puccini or Callas you like?"

"Callas. I have a weakness. I fall in love too easy. When I was fourteen, I fell in love with Maria Callas. You listen to her and you can't conceive how so much beauty can come from one single person. It's her soul that's singing."

"Did you fall in love with Kate?"

She raised her shoulders a fraction of an inch. "I tried not to. I knew it would be trouble."

"Trouble?"

"She was beautiful inside." Her eyes met mine. "She was nice to look at, but inside, she was beautiful. Everyone in the world except her could see she was a lesbian. Just like everyone except her could see she was in love with Jane. I didn't stand a ghost of a chance."

"But she did fall for you."

She took a pull on her whiskey and savored it before swallowing.

"It's not that simple, Stone."

"Explain it to me. I'm here to find the truth."

"Yeah?" She laughed. "You're the one cop in the world who's interested in the truth?" She sighed. "The truth. I'm a man, Stone. Whatever operations I have or may have had, I'm a man. But you know the problem? I hate men. I've been beaten, I've been abused, I've even been raped, all by men. But I love women. I love women so much the only way I could find peace with myself was by pretending I was one. And you're right, I fell in love with Kate. But Kate was a lesbian. A real lesbian. Most gays and lesbians are ambiguous, you know what I mean? But Kate was an actual lesbian."

She stopped talking, staring at the floor. I frowned, beginning to understand and fill in the blanks.

"You had the operation for Kate? You didn't have it before?"

Her voice was barely a whisper. "I had the operation for Kate. When I came over from Cali, I started taking the pills for the boobs so I'd stop seeing a guy when I looked in the mirror. But I didn't like how they made me feel. So sometimes I took 'em and sometimes I didn't. My doc used to get crazy with me. But I did what the hell I liked, like I always did. But then Kate and I started getting close, you know?" She looked at me, like she wanted to know I understood what getting close was. "And she said, she told me, maybe if I went the whole way, maybe if I became a woman, it could happen between us. So I had the operation."

"Who was your doctor?"

She looked at me like I was nuts. "That makes a difference? That matters?" I didn't answer. I waited. She sighed. "Dr. Weiss, 169th and Franklin, in Morrisania."

"You want to tell me about the letters?"

"Not really."

"Did Kate get them for you?"

"Yeah. Whatever."

"What did you want them for? Did you already know you were going to kill her?"

"I guess I must have."

"Why? Because you knew she was really in love with Jane?"

She bit her lower lip. She took a couple of deep breaths through her nose, then said, "No. That wasn't it. She was moving on from Jane. What we had was getting stronger."

"Why then?"

"You wouldn't understand, Stone, and even if you did, you wouldn't believe me."

"Where's the typewriter?"

She put down her glass. "Let's get this over with, Stone. You got your DNA, what more do you want?"

"I want the typewriter, I want to know how you got the letters, and I want to know why you killed Kate."

"Where's your partner? Dehan? She's cute. I'll tell her."

I shook my head. "No, you tell me."

"You've got my confession, and you've got my DNA. You want me to get deep and talk about why I done it, I talk to Dehan. You're a nice guy, Stone. You're probably one of those few decent guys. But you're a man, and I hate men. I'll talk to Dehan. She's cute. Where is she? How come you came alone?"

I went to stand. "You can talk to her at the station. Let's go."

"I'm right here." I turned. She was in the doorway looking down at me. She gave her head a small shake that said we'd discuss it later. "So talk, Bella. Where's the typewriter, how did you get the letters, and why did you kill Kate?"

Bella stared at her for a moment with no expression on her face. Then she shook her head. "You are one beautiful woman. You look the way Maria Callas sounds." She gave a small shrug. "Why did I kill Kate? Let me show you."

She reached down beside her among the cushions on the chair. What she pulled out was a Taurus G2C 9mm semi-automatic. She pointed it at me but spoke to Dehan.

"Come inside and close the door."

TWENTY

Dehan stepped in and closed the door behind her.

"You're making a big mistake, Bella."

"Save it, sweet cheeks. You grow up my side of the tracks, you learn there are two kinds of people you can never trust: cops and everybody else." She swung the gun so she was aiming straight at Dehan's gut. She spoke to me. "Drop your weapons on the sofa, and you, Stone, get face down on the floor with your hands behind your head."

I didn't move. "Leave her out of it, Bella. Let her go, and you and I can talk."

"Do that one more time, Stone, and I will blow a hole the size of a grapefruit through her belly. Get on the floor."

I held up my hands. "Okay, Bella, I am going to cooperate. Nobody needs to get hurt here."

I lay on the floor and sensed her getting to her feet.

"Worst thing you can do right now, Stone, is patronize

me. I am scared, and I am mad. So you really don't want to upset me."

"You're scared?" I gave a small laugh. "You're holding a gun on my partner, and I am face down on the floor. You want to take a guess at how I feel?"

"Stop, you're breaking my heart." Then she added, "You, get on your knees."

I heard a stifled squeal from Dehan and a violent scuffle. My belly burned, and I was pushing myself up when a boot landed on my back and pushed me down again.

"*Stay down!*"

I said, "Bella, I need you to listen to me. I came here to talk to you. I could have stormed this place and taken you in, but I needed to talk—"

"Shut up! You planted my DNA and now you want to send me away! It ain't gonna happen, cop!" There was a moment's silence. Then in a more controlled voice, "I am going to tell you what is going to happen next."

I interrupted her. "Why didn't you kill me at Silva's place?"

She was quiet for a long moment, then snarled, "Shut the fuck up, Stone. You reach in your pocket and you take out your cell. You call off the boys in blue outside. Then you call your chief at the station and you tell him new evidence has emerged and you are following up a lead. You will be in touch."

"You're out of your mind. It will never work."

I head Dehan scream through gritted teeth, then Bella's voice. "Shut the fuck up!" Silence, then, "You call your *fuckin'* chief. *I* will decide what will and will not work! *Understood?*"

"Yes."

"After you have called off your dogs and your chief, you will call the goddess Jane Morley, and you will tell her to come here, with Danny fuckin' Santos, in the Bentley. And then the four of us, Jane and Danny and Dehan and me—you're not included in this party, lover boy, sorry. You get to stay behind and convince everybody else not to come after us. Because if I smell a cop, if I smell a piece of dog shit that reminds me of a cop, Detective Dehan dies slowly and painfully."

I heard another repressed screech of pain and Bella's "Make the call, asshole."

I came up on one elbow and reached in my jacket for my cell and called dispatch. I called and gave my name and badge number. "I'm at Norton and Turneur with Weller and Joyce waiting outside in a patrol car. I need you to call them off."

There was an edge of pissed irony in the dispatcher's voice when she answered, "Detective, can you not follow the standard procedure of stepping outside and telling them yourself?"

"No, I can't do that. Will you please just convey my message to them?"

Her tone changed. She had picked up something was wrong. She said, "Yes, Detective, I'll do that for you."

"Thanks."

Bella's voice came to me. "Now your chief."

"I'm on it, Bella. Take it easy."

"Tell me that one more time and I swear—"

"It's ringing."

"Put it on speaker."

"He'll notice, and he'll get suspicious."

I heard the superintendent's voice in my ear. "John, you have her in custody? What is happening?"

"Sir, some new evidence has emerged. I can't tell you what it is right now. I am about to follow it up. I'll be in touch shortly. I've sent Weller and Joyce back to the station."

"John, what on Earth…?"

"Yup, that's what it looks like. I'll be in touch as soon as I have something."

The last thing I heard was the chief saying, "But, but…"

"Okay, now what?"

"You know what. Call Jane."

I dialed. It rang five times before it was answered. Then there was silence for three or four seconds.

"John…?"

"Yeah."

"What is it? Have you found Bella?"

"Yeah, listen, I need to ask you and Danny a favor. The DNA tests link her unequivocally with Silva's death."

"Oh my God! But why? What on Earth could she have against poor Henry?"

"I need you to listen, Jane. There is no error in the DNA. It's conclusive. She killed Silva. We are at her house, and we have her in custody. But we are having trouble with something."

"What? Is she there with you?"

"No, Dehan and the uniforms have her in the living room. The problem I have is linking her with Kate's death. With no typewriter, the link I have is tenuous at best. She says she's willing to talk to us without a lawyer, but only if you and Danny are present."

"But why?"

"She says you're the only person she trusts. Jane, honestly, I think she believes if you hear her story, you might foot the bill for a good attorney. But I really need you to do this for me. We need a confession regarding the Kate Hagan murder."

"Can't you just prosecute her on Silva's murder?"

"No, a good attorney could use that to make the whole case seem unsafe."

It was bullshit, but it was all I had. After a moment, she said, "All right. Give me half an hour."

I forced a smile into my voice. "Do me a favor. Are you coming in the Bentley?"

She laughed. "I can, why?"

"Dehan always wanted to ride in a Bentley. She asked me to ask you."

She laughed again with genuine pleasure. "Well, tonight her wish will be fulfilled!"

I hung up and turned to look at Bella. She was staring at me hard.

"You are one subtle, devious son of a bitch."

"Let Dehan go. You have me and America's sweethearts as hostages, for crying out loud. Let her go."

"No way. I came close to thinking you could be trusted at the beginning. You have this good-guy look and manner. But you're just a dirty cop like all the rest." She gave a small laugh. "You think I don't know? Does Detective Dehan know?"

Dehan was frowning at me. "Know what?"

"That this guy and the goddess Jane Morley were lovers. Did you know that?"

I looked Dehan straight in the eye. "It's not true. We met at a party, years ago, but that was all."

Dehan's face had gone blank. She said, "I should care?"

Bella squinted at her like she was stupid and gestured at me. "He's dancing to her tune—"

I cut across her. "Where is the typewriter, Bella? What did you do with it?"

"Enough with the fuckin' typewriter, Stone!"

"How did you get the letters? It was stupid to leave your DNA at the scene, but you know, don't you, that if they connect you with Kate's murder, you'll never set foot outside a prison for the rest of your life. You need to cooperate with me, Bella. There is no way you can get away with this. You *need* to cooperate. Where is the typewriter?"

"*I don't have a fuckin' typewriter! Who has a fuckin' typewriter these days? What's the matter with you?*"

"How did you get the letters?"

She rammed the semi-automatic into the back of Dehan's head and screamed, "Say it! Say it one more time! Ask it one more fuckin' time!"

I held up my hands. "I'm sorry. I am genuinely trying to help you."

"By framing me, you son of a bitch?"

There was a rap at the door and the ringing of the doorbell. Bella scowled at me. "They didn't make it from Manhattan in ten minutes."

I shrugged and raised myself from one elbow into a sitting position. "She didn't say where she was. She just said they'd be here soon. It might be Weller and Joyce wanting confirmation. Cops don't like it when you stray from procedure."

She stared at me for a long moment. The doorbell rang again, and there was more hammering.

"Go talk to them. One slip, one false move, and you'll see just how beautiful she is on the inside."

I stood and glanced at the sofa. Our weapons were not there. I opened the door, and she said, "Leave it open."

She had her gun to Dehan's head. Dehan was kneeling on the floor.

"My knees are hurting. Can I sit?"

I didn't hear the answer. I made my way down the hall toward the door. Behind me, I heard Dehan say, "I'm pregnant," and Bella expostulate, "Holy shit!"

I opened the door. It was Weller and Joyce, frowning. Weller started to say, "What's going on, De—"

I put my index and middle finger under my chin, like the barrel of a gun and said, "Nothing. Everything's fine. Some new evidence has emerged, and I am looking into it. I didn't want you guys hanging around for no reason."

While I spoke, I pulled my cell, found Notes, and typed furiously. I showed the note to Weller and said, "Right now." I paused to give the words effect, then went on. "We have a couple of witnesses showing up in a few minutes, and I want to talk to them. The information couldn't be more important. You guys head back to the station." I shook my head gently, praying to God they'd pick up my meaning. "And the chief will give you instructions. This is just a ten one-oh-eight."

I slipped my finger over my lips and then gestured them to leave. Weller nodded.

"Yes, Detective. I understand. It wasn't standard procedure, so we thought we'd check before leaving. You have a good evening."

"I'll catch you later."

They turned and made their way back toward their car. As I closed the door, I noticed they had started to run and Weller was pulling his cell. I walked back to the living room and paused in the doorway.

"Bella, this is way out of hand. We need to scale down."

"What is a ten one-oh-eight?"

"A situation that has been defused or no longer concerns the cops. Jane and Danny will be here in less than ten minutes. Let's put away the guns and start to deescalate."

"So you can quietly put me away for crimes I never committed?"

"No, so you can explain to me how your saliva came to be on Silva's face."

She looked away in disgust. "Jesus!"

"So you can explain to us why you decided to fake those letters. What were you trying to achieve? Had you already decided to murder Kate? If so, for what reason? Talk to me, Bella!"

She had tears in her eyes. "She's your wife," she said. "She's pregnant."

I shook my head. "Don't do it, Bella. Trust me. We can make this right."

"No, I lost my Eurydice. I lost her a long, long time ago. I was born into failure, lived trying to escape who I am, and what's left for me is a descent into hell. The next forty years of beating and abuse and rape. I don't think so."

"For crying out loud, Bella. Listen to me! Talk to me.

Talk to me about the letters, the typewriter, what was your motive for killing Kate? Talk to me!"

"What is wrong with you? I already told you!"

"*Talk to me!*"

The doorbell rang. We stared at each other. She said, "It's Jane and Danny. Go let them in."

I walked down the hall and opened the door. The big Bentley was parked in the drive, and Jane and Danny were standing on the porch. Jane looked tragic, and Danny looked pissed. Past them, I could see Weller running down the street toward me. He had a cell phone in his hand.

I said, "Jane, Mr. Santos, come in. They are in the living room. Go on ahead."

Weller squeezed past the trunk of the big car and approached me. He handed me the phone. "He's on the line."

I listened carefully, then asked, "Can you confirm that by email?"

He said he could, and I handed him back to Weller to make the arrangements and told him, "Tell the chief I want the cavalry, and I want them now."

I walked back to the living room and drew breath to speak, and froze. Danny was standing paralyzed with a look of horror on his face. Dehan was sitting, cross-legged, very pale and with her eyes closed. Bella was standing with her arm stretched out and her pistol pointed at the back of Dehan's head. Her cheeks were shiny with tears, and her bottom lip was trembling, curling in under her teeth.

Jane was sitting on the arm of the sofa, looking up into Bella's face. Her own was without expression; her lovely blue eyes were cold, dead.

"Bella, you know what you have to do. You have to do the right thing. You know we have talked about this so many times over the years. You can make a wonderful life for yourself, Bella, but you have to do the right thing. And right now, the right thing is to hand over to Detective Stone the typewriter you used to write those letters, tell him how you got hold of the originals, and explain to him what on *Earth* made you kill poor, poor Kate and poor Henry. I will get you the very best legal representation, Bella. I will spare no effort, and we will find some kind of solution. But you must tell Detective Stone the truth."

Bella was sobbing. Her tears were flowing freely, but her hand was not wavering.

"Where is the typewriter, Bella? Is it in your room?"

Bella was shaking her head. "I don't know, I don't know."

Jane turned to Danny. "Go to her room. Have a look." She turned to me. "An Olivetti?"

Danny left the room. Jane kept talking.

"You were in love with her, weren't you, darling? You wanted her to marry you, be your wife, poor Bella. You thought she'd leave me and Danny to be with you. But she refused, didn't she? For her, it was just a flirtation, an exciting game of self discovery, discovering her sexuality, but for you, it was so much more than that, wasn't it? After your troubled past and painful childhood, wasn't it, darling? Another betrayal, another failure, another reason for self-hate. Poor darling Bella."

She turned to look at Jane. Her face was ugly and twisted, her eyes and nose and lips swollen and wet. Her body was swaying, but her gun hand was steady, like that was the pivotal point of her whole life.

I said, "Give me the gun, Bella. I just spoke to your doctor. I know everything." I reached out my hand. "Give me the gun."

It must have been just a fraction of a second, but it became timeless. There was a total stillness in the room and, as though I were looking through a microscope, I saw her finger tighten on the trigger. My mind screamed. I lunged forward, but it was as though I was lunging through invisible molasses. Then there was a flash, and the world exploded.

The room seemed to be spinning. I was deaf, and I felt sick. There was a stench of gunpowder in my nostrils, and the walls wouldn't stop moving.

She was lying on the floor. Her face was screwed up, and under her head, there was a vast pool of slowly oozing blood. I pushed Danny out of the way and reached down for Dehan, who was trembling on the floor, clutching at her stomach.

"It was her, baby. It was her," I said, hearing my own voice muffled as though it were in another room.

I pulled her to her feet, and she clung to me, sobbing into my shoulder. I kissed her head and stroked her hair. She kept repeating, "Stone, I thought she was going to kill the baby. I thought she was going to kill our baby."

As I held her, I became aware of a hammering at the door. A moment later, I heard the door open, Danny's voice, Weller and Joyce, other voices. Then there were people filling the room, all talking at once. I had my eyes closed and was clinging to Dehan's living warmth, listening to her breathe slowly and steadily.

It was the chief's voice that brought me back, unwillingly, to that ugly room.

"John, John, is she all right? Is she hurt? The baby...?" I turned and looked at him. "There's an ambulance outside. We didn't know what to expect. You should let the paramedics look at her."

We reluctantly let go of each other, and I released her into the hands of two paramedics. As I watched her go, I turned and looked down at Jane, still sitting on the arm of the sofa. She was wiping a tear from her eye.

"Jane," I said, "Jane Morley, I am placing you under arrest for the murder of Katy Hagan and Henry Silva. You do not have to say anything, but anything you do say may be taken down and will be used in evidence against you."

EPILOGUE

"You arrested Jane Morley, America's sweetheart, for the murder of her agent and her personal assistant ten years earlier, even though the DNA of the woman who had just shot herself was all over Silva's face and the cable that had been used to strangle him."

As she said this, she dug her toes in the sand at Drake's Beach and sipped her apple juice.

"Yes," I said and nodded. "I did do that, but you see, I knew Bella couldn't have done it."

She showed me a screwed-up, skeptical face, shook her head, and looked out at the sea.

"*How?*" she said with some emphasis. "She was holding a gun to my head, her saliva was all over Silva's face, her skin was ion the cable used to strangle him, she even admitted to you that she'd done it..." She nodded with some sarcasm. "I can see how all of that would lead you to conclude she hadn't done it."

I unlaced my boots and allowed myself an indulgent chuckle. She spoke to the sea.

"Don't you even dream of saying, 'It was too easy.'"

I dug my bare feet into the sand. "Hell, it was anything but that. In fact, it was too difficult. The word that kept nagging at me from the start was 'incongruous.' Two bits of evidence fit, but then there was a third pointing the other way. One piece of evidence was indisputable, but everything else contradicted it. It was incongruous, and then you started with your sexual proclivities."

She arched an eyebrow at me. "Excuse me?"

I ignored her and gave my head a little shake. "And then, nobody had a motive. We had to *invent* motives for our suspects. But this little voice in my head kept telling me the motive in ninety percent of cases, all over the world, is sex."

I paused. The waves sighed and thudded in a slow, wet tattoo.

"Sex, sex, sex... Of course Bella was all about sex on many levels. Her driving force from the age of fifteen, or before, was her deep love and loyalty toward Jane and the deep hatred she felt toward herself and her own sex, a hatred that fueled her devotion. But again, every time I spoke to her, that love and devotion that *could* have been a motive for murder was directed in the wrong direction. She adored Jane but had no illusions about their relationship, and she loved Kate, but both she and Kate knew that the real object of their love was Jane. They were each a consolation prize for each other. At first, at least."

She lifted her shoulders. I watched her and noticed for the first time the small bulge of her tummy.

"But the DNA, Stone. That closed the case for everyone. Except you."

"Yeah, I was lucky. Five seconds before Joe phoned with the results, I had put together my incongruous with your proclivities, and the key to the case—the motive—had dawned on me.

"You see, all Henry Silva had done was remove himself from Manhattan to try and keep a low profile while we were snooping around. The reason for that was obvious: He and Danny and Jane had colluded in presenting false alibis for each other, and that could cause them a lot of trouble, legally and professionally. But as to what he had done the night of Kate's murder, of the three of them, he was the one who actually had a verifiable alibi. His companion that night—"

"His high-class hooker."

"Thank you, had been awake, watching TV. *He* had been asleep. So what reason would Bella—who told us clearly from the start that she knew everything that went on—what reason would she have for assuming that it was him, and not Danny, who killed Kate? Any motive we invented for Silva applied equally to Danny. In fact, we invented *more* for Danny because we had him in a relationship with Kate. But Danny had no alibi. So why go after Silva instead of Danny? It didn't stand up to scrutiny."

She grunted and sipped her juice. "You could have shared these thoughts at the time."

I ignored her again and went on. "And then there was the forensic evidence. None of it made any sense. And the only thing that connected the two murders was that set of slim fingerprints on the letters and on the whiskey bottle. Two murders that were unquestionably linked because of the victim and the timing, had only one *forensic* link: those prints."

She nodded, glanced at me, and said, "Huh."

"But that wasn't all, Dehan. There was *zero* forensic evidence at Kate's murder, but a superabundance at Silva's murder. Yet both were brutal, and both displayed an important feature in the MO."

She frowned. "They did?"

"Yes, and it was very clever. In both cases, the victim was incapacitated before being killed. The detectives in the original case assumed from the brutality of the assault, the broken bones and the violence, that we were dealing with a big, powerful man. But I always wondered, why does a big powerful man incapacitate a woman before killing her? He could have killed her outright. What stopped him?

"And the same was true of Silva. He had been incapacitated with a Taser before he was strangled.

"And then there was the music. That was really incongruous. It was completely at odds with the first murder. There was nothing remotely sentimental about that. It was like all the *obvious* clues were pointing at revenge by Kate's mystery lover, but the more subtle, hidden ones were suggesting it was the same killer."

"Really? You got that?" She puffed out her cheeks and refilled our glasses.

"It was all there, jumbled up, everything contradicting everything else, but yeah, that troubled me.

"Then there was the fact that the letters pointed us so easily toward Bob Newport, but he so obviously wasn't the guy. The fact that the first letters were written by him, but the later, threatening ones were so clearly written by another person—hence the fact that they were typed. How long was it going to take us to work that out?

"So as we had taken the case on the strength of new evidence, we had no choice but to go and start snooping around the studio. And everything we learned there, though it made us look at Danny and Silva, drove us inevitably toward Bella. You said it yourself: 'It was always going to be her.' The whole thing was set up to lead us to Bella."

She shook her head, frowning. "But why? And how could you be so sure? You've been telling me since you picked me up from the hospital that you were going to tell me. I'm still waiting."

"Why? What I figured, and Jane has since admitted in her confession, was that after Bella had seduced Kate and made her admit that she was in fact a lesbian, Kate started an affair with Jane herself."

"With *Jane?* Jane is a *lesbian?* Holy cow!"

"You remember you got mad at me for asking Silva if he thought Jane was unsatisfying? Jane used men, she used her sex appeal and her looks to acquire slaves, but she never enjoyed men. I had always had a hunch she might prefer women. The problem was that Kate was really hung up on Jane, and once they had become lovers, she started making demands that Jane come out and they get married."

Her jaw dropped. "So the king-sized bed she insisted on was for her and Jane!"

"Yup."

"But the brutality of the attack, the broken bones…"

"A woolen sock full of ball bearings."

"Sweet Jesus. And the complete absence of forensics

killed the case." She frowned again. "But then, why get us to reopen it?"

"Because she had got herself into the same problem again, only worse. Bella had always been obsessed with her, since she was a kid. When Kate died, Bella became even more dependent on her, and Bella, who was nobody's fool, started making demands. But not the way Kate had. Bella was as much a ruthless user as Jane was and was making sexual and romantic demands on her. Finally, according to Jane, she started to demand that Jane come out and marry her. If she didn't, Bella would spill the beans to the media. As with Kate, that signed her death warrant. Because it would destroy America's sweethearts."

"So Jane collected saliva and hair from her lover."

"Urgh!"

"Not as hard as you might think. She retyped the letters…"

"Those prints were hers, then?"

"On the letters and on the bottle, yup, and she set up a very subtle frame for Bella."

"But why kill Silva? He was their agent. He had made them millions."

I nodded. "Yeah, I asked her that. Silva reckoned America's sweethearts had seen their day. He wanted to retire them and had even suggested to Jane that in today's gender-fluid culture, it might actually give her career a boost to come out with a girlfriend."

"Wow!"

"So when it dawned on me that if Jane was a lesbian, and there was a powerful, repressed, explosive relationship between her, Kate, and Bella, it reframed the whole dynamic.

Then the evidence began to fall into place. And when Bella told me she had not had the operation until Kate had asked her to, that triggered a memory. I remembered that Jane had told me Bella had been off sick on the night of the gala—the night of Kate's murder. This was a worker everybody agreed was tireless and dynamic and never got sick. So I got her to give me her doctor's number and told Weller to call and get the date of her operation…"

I trailed off, and she stared at me. "Holy cow, Stone."

"Danny was making hay with his sleeping beauties, Silva was sleeping on his beauty's bosom, and Bella was in hospital recovering from her operation. So Jane arranged to slip away from the party and meet her lover for a night of passion. Or that's how she presented it to Kate. Actually she went there to kill her and then persuaded Henry Silva and Danny to collude with her in an alibi, allegedly for *their* protection."

"Holy smokes, Stone. And the typewriter?"

"She had been making the pretence of continuing her affair with Bella, and she had planted the typewriter there. That was partly why Bella was so devastated. She believed Jane was actually in love with her. But Jane was only ever in love with one person."

"You. That's why she didn't kill you at Silva's house."

"Herself, Dehan. Herself."

We were quiet for a while, watching the waves and listening to their slightly irregular hiss and sigh. After a while, she asked, "Are you going to miss all that?"

"I have wondered, but in that moment when I thought Bella was pulling the trigger on you, I knew it had to stop."

She gave a small laugh and leaned against me. "Imagine how *I* felt!"

I smiled. "I did, believe me. Besides, I am writing my memoirs, as you know."

"Are you making progress?"

"I have reached page four. It starts—" I closed my eyes and recited, "Dehan was the best-looking cop in the 43rd precinct. She could have been a model. But everybody hated her because her attitude was as ugly as her face and body were beautiful. She was about five-seven, built like a goddess with long black hair and black eyes, and a face as sullen as a Monday morning hangover."[1]

She thumped me and laughed. "Supermodel! Ha!"

I smiled. "So while you were in the hospital, I bought you the house you wanted."

"You did *what?*"

"The I Ching says Random House are going to give me a huge advance on my memoirs. You want to go and see it? I want to show you the master bedroom and the nursery..."

---

1. See *An Ace and a Pair*

ABOUT US

Right House is an independent publisher created by authors for readers. We specialize in Action, Thriller, Mystery, and Crime novels.

If you enjoyed this novel, then there is a good chance you will like what else we have to offer! Please stay up to date by using any of the links below.

Join our mailing lists to stay up to date --> righthouse.com/email
Visit our website --> righthouse.com
Contact us --> contact@righthouse.com

facebook.com/righthousebooks
x.com/righthousebooks
instagram.com/righthousebooks

Printed in Dunstable, United Kingdom